THE LIE

REBELS OF RIDGECREST HIGH #2

BELLE HARPER

ELEVENTEEN PUBLISHING

Edited By: Autumn Reed

Proofread By: Jade Taggart

Cover By: MerryBookRound

Copyright © 2022 by Belle Harper

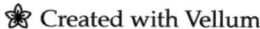 Created with Vellum

BLURB

The Pact is Over.

And the lies keep building.

Hunter:

The Pact is over.

I'm going to make Mila mine.

She will know how much I love her. *Everyday.*

Jace:

I predicted this when I was ten.

Mila Hart destroyed everything.

But I will get it all back…anyway I can.

Roman:

I couldn't protect her.

I almost lost her.

I will never be the man she needs.

Mila:

Everything's changed.

But I will do anything for them.
I will lie...to protect the ones I love.

TW

Hi readers,

I wanted to clear up some possible triggers for The Lie.

Please don't read any further if you don't want to be spoiled.

There is themes of family violence, trauma, anxiety attack, PTSD.

There is a death/murder scene in detail between chapters 23-25

Thank you so much, Belle

ONE

MILA

hate my mom, and there is nothing my dad can say that will ever change my mind. Even though I'm twelve, the fact that I'm moving away makes me want to throw a temper tantrum that would make a toddler proud.

"Honestly, James, the clothes you've given her make her look like a boy. Does she even own any dresses?" Mom lets out a huff. "Don't bother. I will just have to get her something in New York. My daughter won't be seen dead in any of these Walmart clothes."

I don't care what I wear. I like to be comfortable, but I don't dress like a boy. Maybe if Mom were home more, or even took me shopping, she might have a say in what I wear. But Dad took me to pick out my own clothes. I do have a dress. She's just never around to see me, so she doesn't know any better.

"I wanna say goodbye one more time," I whisper to

Dad as I eye Mom going through my closet, throwing clothing and hangers onto my bed. Is it still my bed? If I don't live here anymore? I don't want to think about it. I need to see them. I need one last goodbye.

He looks down at his watch and nods. "Be back at two. Not a minute later."

I glance back at my mom, but she hasn't heard me, and I wouldn't care if she did. I'm leaving with her at two. So, she doesn't get a say in where I go with the last few hours of my life here. I have a plan, something that I'd been hoping to do for a long time. Only, Mom sped up the plans by deciding to take me away. I know what I want before I leave today.

My first kiss.

Running to my bike, I jump on and ride out to the front of my house. I look back at the blue front door and let out a deep breath. Today will be the last day I see that door. My emotions are going haywire, and I don't want to ruin these special last moments with the boys by crying.

Jace's house draws my attention. It looks just like mine, but his front door is green. He's been my best friend since I was born. Choosing Jace for my first kiss would make sense to everyone who knows us...but that's only looking from the outside. Jace won't be my first kiss. I've known that for a while now.

I look down the street to the right—Hunter. With his cheeky smile and floppy curly hair. He always makes me laugh. Makes me feel so special. It would make sense to pick him as my first kiss, right? Wrong.

They'll both kiss me back without question. I know that in my heart. And although I want that—I would hate to be rejected—I know it has to be this way. All three or none at all. And the only wild card I have is…

Roman.

I peddle the wheels of my bike as fast as I can to his trailer, my heart pounding and my stomach tied in knots. What if he doesn't want to kiss me? What if their pact is so strong Roman won't break it and be my first kiss?

The nerves have me almost backing out of my plan. But the fact I don't want it to be anyone else keeps me peddling.

I love all my best friends. But in so many different ways. I usually know what Jace is thinking. How Hunter will react to most things. But Roman? He always leaves me guessing. He makes my chest ache when he's sad and explode when he smiles at me.

My heart always beats a little bit faster for Roman's smiles. Hunter gives me butterflies when he touches me, and Jace makes me feel safe and cared for when he snuggles me. But Roman…he's my wild card. I never know what I'm gonna get with him. I think that's what draws me to him most. The unpredictability.

If he says no to my first kiss, I won't go to the others. It only counts if they're all my first kiss. And I want my real first kiss to be with Roman. I want him to feel the same thing I do in my chest. I want his heart to explode with happiness the way I know it will for me.

I swallow before knocking on his door. Hearing

stomping feet, I take a step back. I lace my fingers in front of me, hoping it's going to be Roman and not his dad. His dad scares me; he always smells bad and smokes inside the trailer.

The trailer is always gross and dirty, but I never say anything or let my gaze linger longer than needed when I'm in there. Not that I'm in there much. Roman hates us coming to his trailer. My dad doesn't like me coming here either. He doesn't like Mr. Valentine.

The door flies open and makes a loud bang as it hits the side of the trailer. I jump at the sound, sucking in a gasp at the sight of Roman's dad. The smell hits me just as fast as he scratches his chest. The stained wifebeater moves under his dirty nails, and I hold my breath.

He looks me up and down. "You're that little girly Roman hangs around. Mia, right?" He lets out a deep, chesty cough. After making a sound in his throat, he spits just near my feet, and I start to shake. Not much scares me, but he always makes something in the pit of my stomach scream at me to run.

"Mila," I correct him, but my voice is almost a whisper.

"Ah, Mila. Pretty name for a pretty girly."

Run! Run!

"Is Roman here?" I ask, my feet already backing up, and I watch as he catches the movement and he cocks his head.

His mouth grows into something I assume would be a smile on a normal person, but on him, it looks evil.

"The kid's not here. He said he was taking off to the lake."

I nodded. Roman's at the lake. That makes sense. Or did it?

"Are you sure?"

He pulls a cigarette from his pack with his teeth and proceeds to jam the packet back in his shorts pocket. His lighter clicks a few times before the flame catches. He lights the end, and it glows brightly as he inhales. Smoke comes from his nostrils like he's an angry dragon.

"Yeah, he said something about you and left." His eyes rake over me again, and I feel a shiver course through my body. Run!

"You can wait here for him; can come sit inside and wait with me." He steps to the side and makes a gesture for me to come in. The hair on the back of my neck pricks in a warning.

I don't want to; that's the last place I want to be. The way he looks at me has my gut screaming. Run!

"No, thank you." I'm polite, at least, before I jump on my bike and ride as fast as I can away from there.

The distance between Mr. Valentine and myself allows me to finally let out the breath I didn't realize I'd been holding in. I can't leave here; I can't leave Roman with that man. He's not a good person.

I ride my bike toward the lake. It's kind of in the middle of us all, that's why we meet there so much. Plus, it's fun to swim there on a hot day. Is he swimming? Alone? That's a rule we have; we can't swim there alone. Someone always needs to be there in case one of us gets into trouble. The other would call for help.

My legs are starting to burn from pedaling so much, but I need to get to him fast. When I reach the grass, I pedal until I see him, sitting on the edge of the lake, throwing rocks into the deep water.

I drop my bike about five feet behind him and he turns, his arm midair, about to throw another rock into the water. As he squints up at me through the sun's bright rays, I can tell his cheeks are wet. He's been crying.

Roman never cries. I've only seen him cry once—when his mom died—and then never again. But here he is, crying. I move swiftly to him, my knees dropping to the warm grass beside him as I take his hands in mine.

"Roman," I let out as a breath. "Oh, Roman." My eyes prick with tears of my own.

He pulls a hand away to swipe at the tears. His dirty-blond hair is falling in his eyes, and I reach up and brush it back.

"You need a haircut." I smile at him, and he shakes his head. I brush it back again so I can see his whole face.

"No, I don't want one."

I tilt my head and give him a small smirk. "Why not?"

He always has long hair, and it's forever getting in his eyes and hiding his beautiful face. I want everyone to see Roman and how he's just a boy. A person. Human. Someone worthy of love.

I love him...but I'm going away. I need someone to love him while I'm gone.

"Because if I do, you won't push it away. I like that...I like that you want to."

My heart beats faster in my chest. I want to cry at what I'm losing here; I want my mom to know she isn't only breaking my heart. She's also breaking the heart of this sweet, beautiful boy with the sad blue eyes and dirty-blond hair.

He needs someone to push his hair out of his eyes for him. I don't think he would let the guys do it. It wouldn't be the same. It has to be me. I want it to only be me.

"I came looking for you. I want to ask you a question." *I swallow the lump in my throat as I steady myself to ask this important question.*

He nods, then looks around us. For what, I don't know.

"Would you, Roman Valentine, be my first kiss?"

His blue eyes snap back to mine, wide and full of surprise. His mouth opens slightly as he licks his lips. I smile and nod, trying to hold myself together while waiting for his answer.

"You want me to kiss you...first?"

I giggle and shove him gently in the shoulder, my nerves getting the better of me. "Of course I do, Roman. I want you to be my first kiss."

Roman looks down at my lips then back into my eyes. "Are you sure? Wouldn't you rather Jace or Hunter be your first?"

I shake my head. "You don't want to kiss me?" My belly twists in knots as I wait for his response.

He shakes his head, and I can feel his fingers tremble

where our hands still touch. "No, I mean, yes. I do want to kiss you. I want my first and my last kiss to be with you, Mila."

"I want that too."

I lean into him and close my eyes. I feel his fingers brush over my face. I hold still, confused at what he's doing. He traces around my forehead and down my cheek, and I smile at the way he's tracing my face. It's not what I expected. I guess I didn't know what to expect, but this isn't it.

I'm just about to open my eyes when I feel his warm, callous palm cup my cheek, and I lean a little into it. His breath fans out over my lips. I wait for what feels like a lifetime for Roman's lips to touch mine. The first touch is soft and tender. My hand reaches out and grabs his tee to stop myself from falling over. I need something to keep me grounded.

I'm kissing Roman Valentine.

He presses his mouth harder to mine, and we stay like that as fireworks go off in my head, my heart, and my tummy. It's the best feeling, and I don't want to pull away.

But the wind tumbles my hair and we pull back to look at each other. My heart is racing in my chest as I touch my lips, just as Roman does the same. The smile he gives me lets me know he feels the same thing inside him as I do right now.

"Mila?" my dad's muffled voice calls out to me.

I turn to my bike, then back to Roman, but Dad isn't there. I look at the ground and see daisies scattered on his *mother's grave. How am I at the cemetery? Where did the lake go? I blink and shake my head; I see Roman that first day of first grade. Standing there, looking at me with those big sad eyes, obviously scared and alone. My heart starts to race.*

"Roman? What's happening?"

"Mila? Sweetheart, can you hear me? Come back to me, baby girl."

Dad? I look around and everything is dark. So dark...I can't find Roman. My heart races even faster. Where is he? Where's Roman? He would never leave me.

"Roman?" *I call out. My head pounds and my stomach rolls. And not in a good way.*

"Mila?" *Dad calls out again, and I hear a rhythmic beep. What is that? It starts to speed up, and I grow more anxious at the sound. That's not my alarm clock. The smell isn't of daisies and fresh grass. It's sterile, like a hospital. My hand reaches out, and someone takes it. I can feel their touch. Roman?*

"Open your eyes, sweetheart. Come back to me."

"Dad?" I hear my voice as a strangled whisper, my throat raw and dry.

Then, everything comes rushing back. Roman. My bike. The bad guys from the fight. Their car.

The kiss.

My eyes open, and the light is blinding. With a moan, I close them again and try to stop my stomach from revolting.

"Mila?"

Taking a deep breath, I blink a few times. I look around the cold, white room. There's a lady standing beside me, my wrist in her hand as she looks down at me, smiling.

"Mila? How do you feel?" she asks. I don't know who she is.

I turn to see Dad. He blinks back tears, and it makes my throat close. Kate is there beside him, and she smiles and reaches out to my hand that's gripped tightly in Dad's.

"Mila, hi, sweetheart. Do you need water?" She looks over to the nurse, but I shake my head and groan. It feels like my brain isn't attached and is just bouncing off the inside of my skull.

"What do you need?" Dad asks.

"Roman."

I need Roman.

TWO
HUNTER

Asher clasps his hand on my shoulder in the waiting room, and I jump a little, looking up from my phone. I've been playing Candy Crush and trying not to think about being here...in the hospital.

"She's awake." He smiles as he hands me a bottle of water.

Letting out a sigh of relief, I take the water from him. I've been sitting in this waiting room for hours. The same one I've been in and out of since they brought her here. I know every scuff mark, every crack in the paint, and I'm now on a first-name basis with one of the janitors. Joseph is a great guy, loves the Rebels.

But they'd said today's the day; they were waking her up out of her medical-induced coma. I needed to be here for her when she woke up, but it's immediate family only. Even Asher didn't get that privilege. Only his mom and Mila's dad, James. But they've kept us updated at every stage.

"Is she talking? Does she seem fine?"

He looks down at his phone, and I watch impatiently as he types out a message to his mom. I take a large mouthful of water and force it down. The lump in my throat from worrying that something will go wrong just won't go away. Even with the water. After a moment, he smiles and looks down at me and nods.

"Yeah, Mom said she is fine. But asking for Roman."

Fuck.

"I don't know where he is."

And that was the honest truth. He discharged himself days ago, against doctors' orders, and he went home. But when I went to his trailer to check on him, he wasn't there, and he hasn't been answering any of my messages or calls.

"We'll find him." Asher nods from where he now sits beside me.

"Am I allowed to see her?"

"Yeah, they said to grab some lunch and come back in an hour. They'll let us in then."

I get up and follow the signs to the hospital cafeteria. The food tastes like shit, but I've worked out what *not* to buy now. Asher comes up on my left, and we walk the hallway together.

It's amazing how close Asher and I have become

this past week. Like, I want to kick his ass on the football field still, but he really has Mila's best interests at heart. Hell, we all beat the shit out of that scumbag for Mila. He's a good guy.

He's been passing messages on to me when he hears anything from James. Been letting me know how Mila is, even when I'm at home and worried.

I knew she had some internal bleeding and lots of cuts and bruises.

Roman's face was almost unrecognizable after that beating, and everyone assumed he'd been hit by the car, like Mila. I heard he tried to avoid going to the hospital, but he wouldn't leave Mila's side, and that's how the paramedics convinced him to go.

When I saw him, he looked almost dead, and I was certain that if he hadn't gone with her, he wouldn't be here with us anymore.

Roman wouldn't tell me exactly what had happened, but I've worked out enough to know that the car accident wasn't an accident at all. That the guys who did this to him were the same ones who hit Mila. And he's been blaming himself ever since. I want to find them, to kill them...

Except, I'm worried Roman might have already done that. And maybe that's why I can't find him—he's gone off the grid. Not because they got to him first. I refuse to consider that possibility.

God, I hope you're okay, Roman. Or I will kill you myself.

"Who are you playing tomorrow?" I ask Asher, trying to forget about Roman for a moment. I don't want that on my mind when I get to see Mila. I can't wait to see her, hold her hand in mine and verify that she's okay.

It's Thursday, and even though I've barely been at school this week, there's no way in hell I'm playing tomorrow. My head's not in the game. My heart is lying in a hospital bed, and I need to be with her. But my whole team is playing for Mila. They're good guys...except one.

Jace hasn't been here once. Hasn't messaged me to ask how Mila is. Hell, he didn't even ask about Roman. I'm done with his selfish shit. The only people who deserve my time are Mila and Roman. I'm not chasing after him to tell him how she is, he should be here. I don't care anymore what he does, he's no friend of mine.

"North Point Royals." Asher doesn't seem too enthusiastic.

James and his mom want him to play. He does, too, but I can tell he's conflicted over the whole thing. So, the fact that she's waking up today will be good for him. He's been struggling with Mila being here as much as I have.

I shake my head and clap my hand on his shoulder just as he did to me earlier. He's roughly the same height as me, and he turns to face me. His eyebrows raise, and he gives me a puzzled look.

I chuckle. "Good luck, man. You're gonna need it."

"Hell nah, don't need any luck. We kicked your asses. The Royals are nothing." Asher does some really bad karate moves in the air, and a nurse glares at him as we pass her.

I laugh, because that's a bit of an exaggeration —"*kicked your asses.*" I think he means we kicked *his* ass. "Hope they don't kick your ass, not like Grady did."

"They don't think I'm fucking their girl, so I should be safe."

An older woman gasps, her hand flying to her chest at what Asher just said. Laughing, I grab his tee and drag him faster. In less than an hour, I will be seeing Mila, and I don't want to be kicked out because Asher has a dirty mouth.

"She wants to see Roman. But if you don't know where he is, then I don't stand a chance of finding him." James runs his hands through his hair. "I've been so worried about Mila, I let him slip past. I wouldn't have let him leave."

"I don't want her worried about that right now, either. I'll find him," I reassure James.

James has dark shadows under his eyes, and his

cheekbones are sharper than usual. He looks like he hasn't eaten in a few days, and it's obvious the stress has taken a toll on him.

"Don't get her all riled up, Asher. She needs to rest." His mom pins him with a look.

He puts his hands up and points to himself. "Me? I don't know what you're talking about."

His mom just makes a sound that lets him know she doesn't believe that. I don't have time to think about what she meant by "riled up." I'm only feet away from my girl.

As we walk past them both and head toward the room Mila's in, I shoulder-check Asher.

"Hey, what the fuck?" he calls out, and a nurse glares at us.

"What did your mom mean by riling her up? You into her?" Okay, so I couldn't let it go. Is he into Mila? Not that I blame him. Anyone Mila encounters is drawn into her orbit. It's just who she is. But, fuck him, she's mine. He better not be into her.

He put his hands up defensively and shakes his head. "No, nothing like that. Just, when we're together, we seem to cause havoc. Mostly at home. Just ragging on each other, riling her up, and she riles me up too, man. Just Mila being Mila is all. Nothing else."

Sounds like Mila. After being around Asher all week, I've noticed they are very similar in their personalities. So, I can imagine them messing around like that. But I still don't like it. I give her butterflies. She said that. Does he give her butterflies too? He better not, or I will have to kick his ass.

Shaking my head to clear those thoughts, I put on a smile as I walk into the room and see her. She's so tiny in such a huge bed. Her eyes meet mine, and she smiles at me. My heart's in my throat at the sight of her. She has dark and yellowing bruises and only a few scrapes, but several are deep enough that they will leave scars. Knowing Mila, she will call them *battle wounds*, and she'll be even hotter than before by owning them.

I make my way slowly toward her, not breaking eye contact and trying to smile like everything's okay. It will be. She's alive. She's going to be fine.

The door clicks shut as Asher makes his way up behind me.

"Hey, how are you feeling?" I ask her.

"Like I got hit by a car," Mila deadpans back at me.

I stop and my eyes widen. Asher lets out a huge, bellowing laugh, and I laugh too. Mila will be more than fine. Even though she lies broken on a hospital bed, she's still the feisty Mila we know and love.

"If I'd known that's all I needed to break the tense atmosphere, I would have told my dad the same thing when he asked how I felt."

Moving away from Asher and as close as I can to Mila, I smile down at my girl.

She's gonna be mine.

"Well, if you had, he would've known you're just fine. Smart-ass and tough as nails."

She holds up her right arm to display a blue cast. "Not that tough. I broke my wrist. I have to wear this for six weeks. Or maybe it's only five now. I'm confused by the whole *I've been sleeping for days* thing." She looks over to the door then back to me, her eyes darting between Asher and me.

"When do you get to go home?" I ask. I know who she's looking for, and I quickly change the subject so I don't have to tell her Roman isn't coming.

"If everything goes well, I can leave here in a few days and continue to rest at home. They said they kept me under the meds longer because of something…I can't remember, but it's all good now."

She throws her hands in the air, the one with the cast wobbling a little from the weight. Then she places them down on her blanket and stares at it for a moment.

"I didn't get hit too hard. Or I have a hard head… I don't know, but I'm hoping to go home Sunday. Thank you for coming to see me."

I nod and reach for her hand. She sighs at the contact. "Mila," I bend over and press my lips gently to her forehead, where there aren't any cuts or bruises. "I've been here every day waiting to see you. I wouldn't not be here. They had to drag me home."

When I draw back, I see her eyes. Since I don't

want her to cry, I reluctantly let go of her hand so Asher can get closer to her and give her a break from me for a moment.

"You gonna watch my game tomorrow? Cheer me on? Mom will come back with your dad and Madison later. They'll bring your laptop so you can watch Netflix and me."

She smiles. Good, that cheered her up a little more.

"Oh, Asher...that's a hard one. Netflix or you? Mmm...who are you playing?"

I give her a cocky grin and wink. "Royals."

Asher just shakes his head and grunts something under his breath at me.

"Their quarterback is hot. And they're an amazing team. They are so gonna go to state." She turns to me. "No offense, Hunter. The Rebels are good, but have you seen the Royals?"

I laugh at the sound that escapes Asher's lips. Mila, the shit-stirrer. I see what Kate is talking about now. Riling him up.

"Hey, we have Walker, and you said he is hot. Plus, he's been calling me every day to see how you are. We're all playing for you tomorrow, Mila."

Her hand goes to her chest.

"Aww...you're playing for me?" She beams. "Walker is hotter." Raising her cast up in the air, she says, "Go Kings," and winks at me.

Asher whoops loudly, his fist punching the air.

"I knew I just had to dangle the right incentive to get you cheering for the Kings every week." Asher turns to me. "No offense, man, you're good and all… but Walker's hot. You heard it from the source. Plus, he's a better quarterback than Jace."

Walker Murphy's a cocky guy; he knows he's good. But he's also a decent human too. He cares enough about Mila that he sent her flowers. They're with all the rest that are now at her house since there were too many in the hospital room.

Not like Jace Montero. Not even once has he thought about anyone but himself. The rest of his family has. Grady's been here with me during the week, and his parents have been cooking for James. But not Jace. He's been off with Britney and not giving one shit that Mila's in the hospital.

"Hunter?" Mila reaches out to me as a nurse walks in.

"I need to check her vitals, and she needs a rest, boys. Say your goodbyes."

It isn't enough time. I can't leave her; she's so small and needs me. She needs someone with her. She's strong and so feisty, but it doesn't mean she doesn't need or want someone to take care of her. Shoulder some of the pain. Even if it's to just sit here and listen to her talk or hold her hand.

But I see the way her eyelids droop a little. She is keeping herself awake for us, and I know she needs rest. As soon as I have the opportunity, I will stay and sit with her while she sleeps.

Asher is already tugging on my arm as the nurse gives us a warning look to say goodbye. "I gotta go, beautiful. But I'll be back tomorrow."

"Roman?" she asks, her eyes wide and pleading.

God, if I could bring him to her, I would. I give her a small smile and shrug. I know it's not what she wants to hear. I don't want to lie to her, either, and say he will be here. It's the million-dollar question everyone seems to be asking.

Where's Roman?

THREE
MILA

My house looks like a florist shop. I didn't get to go home Sunday. Or Monday. When the doctor said a *few* days, I thought three. I'd been hoping for two, but here I am, Tuesday, and finally home.

"What the—?" Dad helps me as I step into what I thought was my bedroom, but it doesn't look the same. I straighten and look around. The room has undergone a makeover. Like, a huge makeover. I do a double take because it's so different and in the best way.

"Do you like it?" Dad asks warily.

Tears spring to my eyes. "Like it? I love it."

My old childhood bed has been replaced by a queen-size with a dark walnut headboard. The quilt is plain black, and there are scatter pillows in pink and blue, giving color to the otherwise dark bed. It looks fantastic.

The walls are still white, but they now display old photos I hadn't seen in years in black frames. A blue lamp sits on my new desk, which is a matching dark walnut, and the desk chair is a white leather. Everything looks so different but so...perfect.

Except the strange table sitting to the side. That doesn't belong here. It doesn't match the rest of the room. I point at it, and Dad chuckles.

"Oh, that's not going to stay. Borrowed it from a friend. It's just like the hospital one." But I realize it's a little harder to move on the carpet as I watch him push it over to the bed.

I hug him. It hurts, but he is gentle. "I love this, Dad. Thank you." I swipe the back of my hand over my eyes to stop the tears from falling.

"I wanted to do it when you got back, but then so much was going on that it slipped my mind. I hope you like it. Kate and Madison helped with the colors. Asher and Walker helped carry it all up here while I was with you. They put the desk and bed together and set it all up without me."

"So, if it falls apart in the middle of the night, I need to blame Asher and Walker is what you're saying?"

Dad chuckles. "I'm just so glad to have you home, Mila. You scared me so much; I thought I had lost you."

I hug him again, sad that I made him feel like that. He already lost me once when Mom took me to New York. Which reminds me...

"Does Mom know? Did she call?" I held my breath, waiting for the answer.

"I called her and told her"—he holds the bridge of his nose—"and there is no excuse for her to not come here. But she said she had to think of the baby and that the flight would cause too much stress. She said she would call you once you woke up, but..."

He gives me a small smile and mouths, "Sorry," as he kisses my head.

I feel bad that Dad has to tell me that. I'm not sure what I thought Mom would do but doing nothing seems to have answered that question. She knew I was in a coma and still didn't see me or call me. I feel bad for the poor child she's bringing into this world. No one deserves to be treated like that; she's a shit mom to me. I don't see her improving for any new children.

"Let's get you into your new bed. The mattress is soft and so comfortable."

Dad helps me into bed, and he's right, the mattress is soft and so much better than the old one. He sets up my laptop on the odd little table so I can watch all the Netflix I want.

"Now, call me if you need anything, and I'll come right away." He lifts a bell from the nightstand that also matches the dark walnut furniture. He rings the bell and I laugh.

"Rest, and I will make us a late lunch." He walks out, leaving the door open. To hear my bell, I guess. Sinking deep into the mattress, I close my eyes.

◖▦◗ ◖▦◗ ◖▦◗

"*W*ell, *hello there, angel.*"

My eyes fly open, and I jerk up in bed, my body protesting at the sudden movement. I gasp for air, my heart racing a million miles a minute. That voice...*his face.*

The cops had been to question me, but I knew if I told them where I'd been and who had hurt me that Roman would get in trouble. I couldn't do that to him. Even though I haven't heard from him since I woke up. No one has.

Hunter told me that they're out looking for him. I need to get well again so I can look for him too. Would the guy who hit me...would he be back? Does he have Roman?

I let out a loud sob as my heart starts to break for him all over again. Where's Roman? He needs me. He's hurting, he has to be, and he's hiding like a wounded animal would. He needs help. Deep in my chest, I can feel that he needs me. *Us.*

"Mila? Mila, sweetheart." Dad runs into the room, his eyes wide and unsure of what to do. His hands hover over me, he doesn't know how to help me.

I give him a sad smile, tears flowing and my throat tight with worry. "I'm okay, I just worry about Roman. He's out there all alone; he needs someone, and I'm worried he's lost. I need to go find him. I will keep him safe."

Closing my eyes, I put my hands to my face, the edge of the cast smacking my cheekbone which makes me cry harder. Not at the pain, but at the reminder that, while I'm here, Roman could be in real trouble, and there's nothing I can do about it.

I eventually cry myself to sleep as my dad holds me.

Dad has to help me move around the house, it's part of the doctors' orders. Someone needs to be here to help me for at least the first week. And knowing my dad, he is taking that job extra seriously.

The stairs hurt more than I wanted to admit when I got home, so being confined to my room is good enough for me. The only crap thing is Dad has to be there all the time...like, even when I go to do my business, he is right outside the door.

I told him I will call out when I'm done, but he is so worried that he spends the whole time asking me if I'm okay just on the other side of the door. *Over and over*.

I'm hoping to sneak in there by myself when he goes to work. He needs to go to work. I don't care what the doctors say, I'm fine on my own for a few hours.

"Do you want some tuna casserole that Ella made?"

I shake my head. That's one thing Dad has been doing all day—feeding me meals that people have cooked for us. Ella popped over earlier to see how I am and to take requests. I asked for her fish tacos. The way she cooks them, they're amazing. She said she will have them ready for tomorrow night's dinner and to expect Grady to be the one here eating them with me, since they are his favorite.

It made me happy to know I would be seeing Grady. He brought a care package over while I was sleeping earlier. It's full of chocolate and a card with a puppy on it. Inside, it read, "Get well soon, Mimi. Love, your Rebel in red. Go Rebels."

I chuckled at that. I think Asher might have given everyone the idea that I'm a King supporter now. I did watch the Kings play...and like I said, the Royals were better. But I also watched the highlights of the Rebels game. They didn't do well missing two of their star players. I could see the frustration on Jace's face.

But it wasn't enough to feel sorry for him. *Fucking dick!*

I turn on my laptop and look for something I can binge-watch while relaxing for a few hours. Something mind-numbing that will distract me from Jace and, especially, from Roman.

"What are you watching?" Dad asks, a bottle of water in his hand. When he passes it to me, I look at the two other bottles he brought me earlier that sit untouched.

I hold in a frustrated sound. I love my dad, and I know I scared him, but he's hovering. I get it, but I need time to breathe too. I swear, he just finds reasons to keep coming in here.

"It's some murder show." I take a small breath and let it out. I shouldn't be upset that my dad wants to make sure I'm okay and spend time with me. I guess after four years of not having anyone to hold my hair back when I was sick or care if my day was good or not, it makes moments like these overwhelming instead of comforting. Mom ruined everything taking me away from here.

"Oh yeah?" he replies and just stands there, looking at the laptop screen as it shows an actress in a reenactment of the real-life woman putting antifreeze in a cup that she will hand to her actor husband in a moment.

"It's a true crime thing. Netflix suggested it because I watched that Zac Efron as Ted Bundy movie yesterday. It's about women who kill their lovers. It's interesting. I put it on more for a background noise, but I'm glued to it. She kills not one but two husbands with antifreeze."

"Is that right?"

I turn and see Dad nodding his head, probably thinking I'm crazy. Not that I blame him. I never thought this would be so fascinating. I only watched the Ted Bundy thing because I was having a bit of a *Zac is a hottie* moment yesterday.

I feel the bed dip as Dad sits and stares at the screen while the woman gives her actor husband the cup full of the antifreeze and he drinks it.

T wo hours later, Dad and I haven't moved. I'm snuggled up to his side and feeling happy to be here with him. It took me a little time to relax, but I love having him here. It feels so good to have my dad back.

"I had no idea they could track your phone like that with cell towers."

Turns out, Dad's really into crimes of passion like me. It's funny, because usually he would be watching game tape from the game on Friday. Especially after the loss to the Royals.

"James? Mila?"

"Kate's here," Dad says. "And hopefully has the pasta and garlic bread with her."

My tummy rumbles at the thought of the food I requested for tonight. The hospital meals weren't great at all…okay, the Jell-O was nice, but I'm craving pasta. She said she would get some for dinner tonight.

"We're up here, watching how women kill their lovers," I call out, and Dad's brows raise at me. I chuckle; it hurts, but I don't care.

"Don't be giving her any ideas, Mila," he jokes as I give him a side hug.

It's gentle, but it hurts like a bitch. I think I've overused my body today. My ribs are a mess. The doctors said I was lucky I didn't break any and puncture my lungs. I have two with hairline fractures, so I have to take it easy. It hurts to breathe, but I've figured out that lying more upright helps ease the pain.

"Your favorite person has arrived to save you." Asher barrels into my room, his hair still wet from his shower after training. He's wearing gray sweats and a black tee. "Hey, Coach Hart." He turns to the laptop to see what we've been watching. "Shit, Mila, you've been torturing the old man with terrible Netflix."

"Language, Asher." Dad sighs as he gets off my bed and stands beside Asher.

Asher clamps his mouth shut. I let out some

giggles before I groan silently to myself, not wanting to worry either of them with how much it hurts to laugh.

"Sorry, Coach, I won't say the 'o' word again, I promise." He does a cross sign over his chest with his finger, and I see my dad's eye twitch. He's trying not to laugh at Asher's antics. It has Asher looking worried, and I hold my hand over my mouth so I don't ruin the moment by laughing and groaning in pain.

"What's the 'o' word—" I can see the wheels turning in Dad's head as he works out what Asher means. "I'm not old. You can give me fifty push-ups for that, Asher."

But you can hear the smile in Dad's voice; he loves having Asher here. He loves Kate, and it's obvious how much Asher respects Dad as he drops to the floor and starts doing push-ups without question. I crane my neck to see him on the floor.

"One, two, three…"

"And, Asher, stop calling me Coach at home. I've told you to call me James."

Dad winks at me as he leaves the room and I smile down at Asher. I watch as his muscles bulge and tense. *Fuck*…my dad loves his mom, and we're friends. He's maybe my future stepbrother. I can't look at him like that.

"You don't actually have to do them. Dad's just joking."

Asher wiggles his brows at me as he continues counting and doing push-ups, looking at me every time he comes up.

He pauses. "I know that"—then continues—"but the drool"—down, then up—"on your chin, Mila"—down and up again—"says otherwise."

I wipe my chin. Drool? He laughs and tumbles to the floor, holding his belly.

"Ugh, you wish." I grab the smaller pink pillow and throw it at him, grunting at the pain. It's a soft throw; I don't have the strength for a harder one.

He catches it and lies gently beside me in Dad's empty spot. It makes me smile that he knows not to jump on my bed, like he has every other time. My body presses up against him, and I feel his warmth. It's nice.

"Let's watch something better than this." He pulls the under-bed table closer and taps on my laptop, starting to scroll through Netflix.

"Do you have any suggestions?" I ask as I move to sit a little higher to help ease my ribs a little.

"Porn?"

My mouth drops open as I stare at him. Dad could have heard him. No words come out. I don't have a comeback for that. That threw me for a loop.

"No, you're right. I'm all the porn you need. Arm porn, chest porn…" He sits up and pulls his tee off and lies back down. He flexes his arms, and I watch as he runs his hand down his chest and abs. Ugh…

why does he have to be so flirty and off-limits? I glance away because I don't need to look at him like this.

"Fucker."

"Mila, here's your— Eww, put your top on, Asher." Madison scrunches her nose at the door while holding a bowl of pasta for me.

"Yeah, eww Asher." I fake the same distaste as Madison, only hers is real.

Asher's cocky grin slips a little, and I can't wipe the grin from my face.

"Lies…All lies." He shakes his head, and I catch him wink at me.

This is the best way to spend the night.

FOUR
MILA

Dad spent all day yesterday with me. He said it was a father-daughter day, that he wanted it to be just us for twenty-four hours. So, we didn't have visitors. My fish tacos didn't come with a side of Grady. I could have cried at that; I'd almost eaten half the stash of chocolates he'd given me, and I wanted to thank him. But nope...Dad sent him home. Even Kate, Madison, and Asher stayed away. I loved Dad, but I needed other humans too.

But today is a fresh new day and one for visitors. Hunter will be coming after training tonight. Dad promised me he could come. I lie and stare at my ceiling. It's boring...I'm so bored. You would think getting to sit around and binge-watch shows would be the best thing that could ever happen. Nope.

There's only so much I can take before going stir-crazy.

I thought I would have a hard time convincing Dad that his job is too important to ignore it completely. They are three games into the season already, with their fourth one this Friday, so he shouldn't miss any more work. I argued that he could leave me alone for a few hours, and I would stay in bed and relax, and that the team needs him.

That last part sealed the deal, and he left me here with strict instructions not to leave bed, and if I need anything, to call him and he will come rushing back.

It's been less than an hour when the front door opens and closes. I groan and cover my eyes with my left arm. Dad didn't last long at all.

I hear him coming up, the squeaky stair at the top letting me know he's almost here. I smile at the sound. You can't be sneaky in this house. My bedroom door is still slightly open, so I hope he will just pop his head in, see I'm fine, and go back to work.

Next week, I hope to go back to school. Though I care about my health, I can't just lie around here all day for another week. I'm on day three, and I already need to escape my room, badly. Plus, I'm getting better. I don't hurt as much today as I did yesterday. And my bruises are practically gone.

I hear the door open, and I smile. "Dad, I'm fine. I told you I would be."

When he doesn't answer, I pull my arm away from my eyes and look over to see…

"Hunter?" *What the hell?*

"In the flesh," he says with his dazzling smile as he waves his hand over his body like he is on display. I'm so happy to see him. But also confused.

"Oh my god, how did you get in this time?" I pull the blanket from my legs and sit up. Swinging my legs over the bed carefully, I place my bare feet on the soft carpet.

With the biggest cocky grin, he holds up a key.

My confusion doesn't fade. "I took the spare key after the last time you got in here." Those memories are good ones too. I smirk at him, and I can see the change of expression on his face as he remembers the same thing.

"Well…I had to see you, and I kind of came over last night. Your dad wasn't impressed. But I guess midnight isn't the best time to make a house call. You were sleeping, but I begged him to let me come over today.

"He gave me the key and said that you really wanted him to go to work today, so he asked if I could check in at lunch and make sure you were fine. And to call him if there are any problems."

My mouth drops open and Hunter comes over, placing a finger on my chin to close my mouth. I smile and let out a little chuckle. That's so not like my dad. Or maybe it is. He doesn't know that Hunter and I have something more than a friendship going on…right?

Hunter and I haven't discussed what this is; hell, we haven't talked about it at all. But I know we're more than we were before. I can feel it in the way he touches me and the looks he gives me. It's like the air is charged when he's around. Now, we're just waiting for one of us to climb over that wall we've both built to stop from being hurt and make it real.

I'd said I wanted them all. All three of them. That I wouldn't choose, and I didn't want them to make me. But after everything Jace did, he isn't even on my radar anymore. He can go to hell, for all I care. I still haven't told Hunter what he did to make me so upset.

But I think I need to tell him, since he seems to think Jace will just "come around." I know that's not true. He's mad at me for kissing Grady and, granted, it's not ideal. But it was one kiss, and it didn't mean anything. Well, it did, and it didn't. Childhood crushes can't live up to what you imagined. That goes for both the Montero brothers now. *Sorry Grady.*

It's not like Jace had told me he wanted to be more than friends. I'm pretty sure he was with Britney when I kissed his brother. So, I don't see why he would be upset about me kissing someone. It's not like he wasn't kissing someone else.

I'm not his girl, and we haven't even kissed. Not since we were twelve. I think I know why I picked him to be last now. Like, subconsciously, I knew I would have my heart broken by him, and I saved the pain by choosing him to be my third kiss. I knew Roman would never break my heart. Not intentionally. He would rather catch all the bullets flying toward me than to ever let me get hit. He always put me first, was always there to catch me.

I made the right choice for him to be my first kiss.

"Hey, you okay? Need some water?" Hunter asks, and I blink up at him. He carefully sits beside me, placing his arm tenderly around my waist and moving into me. I let out a sigh as I rest my head on his shoulder.

"I've been thinking…" I start, and I feel Hunter shake his head.

"You've been thinking? This can't be good for me if you're starting this as soon as I walk in."

With a warm smile, I place my left hand on his cheek and inhale a small breath. Pulling his face to mine, I stare into his deep brown eyes. His hot breath on my lips tickles, and I swipe my tongue to wet them. My heart hammers in my chest as his eyes crinkle at the corners.

They widen slightly as I move in and kiss his soft lips. I pull back to see his expression but, before I can, his hand reaches up and cups my face, bringing me closer to him again.

"Mila," he croaks, his voice rough. He sweeps his tongue over my lower lip, and I part my mouth for him on a small gasp. My tongue meets his as he lets out a deep rumble in his chest. It has me grinning so much that he travels to my throat, kissing and nipping the soft skin there as he moves up to my earlobe.

"Well...I do like that kind of thinking, Mila," he whispers into my ear, and I tremble under his hot lips on my throat again. He moves back to my mouth and claims it like he owns me, and I let him. When we pull away for air, he kisses my nose, and the tingles I feel all over have me biting my lower lip.

"I've wanted to do that since you've been back."

"Me too...but that wasn't exactly what I was going to talk about."

He nods and holds my hands...well, as best he can. I let out a deep sigh and tell Hunter about how Jace found out from Grady about the kiss we shared. And how Jace used the walkie-talkie to broadcast Britney giving him head. Plus, the visual that was even worse.

A vision that I can't erase out of my mind. He could have just told me he was mad and didn't want to talk to me. He didn't need to do something so... fucked up. But the message was clear. He doesn't want to be my friend. Or anything else. We are done.

"Jace is a fucking dick. I knew something was up with him." Hunter shakes his head and swears under his breath.

I look down at my hands. I don't want this to come between them.

"He hasn't spoken to me all week. I didn't play Friday's game, but that's no excuse for the shit he's been pulling." Hunter cups my face again, tilting my head back, his eyes searching mine. "You're more important than football, Mila."

His big dark-brown eyes are full of hope but also sadness. I can see how much Jace is hurting him too. I never wanted this for him.

"Hunter, I've wanted to kiss you so many times. But I also didn't know how to go about it because you aren't the only one...that I want to kiss."

"We all give you butterflies." He moves back a little, scanning my face.

I nod and try to work out what he's thinking. Does he understand what I mean by that? That I won't pick, that I can't. *I just can't.* It would break my heart. I need Roman as much as I need Hunter. Just like I need to breathe.

"Jace is out," he whispers.

I nod, not wanting to say his name again.

"Roman?"

My heart feels like it's in a fist, and I can't breathe when Hunter says his name. I'm so worried about him right now. Swallowing, I nod and tremble in Hunter's arms, worried about where Roman is and who's taking care of him.

"I can't just be yours when my heart is pulled to

him. I know you want to be more with me...I want that too. But if it that means having to choose, I can't...I won't." I whisper the last words; my hands shake in his, I'm worried about what he will say.

It's selfish of me to want them both. I never thought it was possible to have feelings for more than one person like this. Not until I came back and they were all at my house. That's when I realized I couldn't choose. It might not be right, but it's how I feel.

"Roman. He hides behind his grunts. But he loves you so hard, Mila. I can see that, always have. I know it would completely break him if I was selfish and asked you to be mine and mine alone. I couldn't live with myself. I couldn't be happy knowing I hurt him because we both fell in love with the same amazing girl. Same goes for the girl who fell for us."

I let out a shuddering breath and choke back a sob. Hunter is too good for me...they both are. I smile as he wipes away a lone tear. When I press my hand against Hunter's chest, it's hard and warm. Why is this so hard? Why does my heart want them both? *Need them both.*

"Hunter. I want us. I want that with Roman too. I'm so conflicted about what I should do. The easy way would be to walk away and keep you both as friends. But then it's not that easy and I'm being unreasonable. My heart will break every time I see you with someone else. Wishing it was me."

God, why is this so hard?

"Mila, I feel the same. I can't have you with anyone else. I would want to break their face. It's not unreasonable." He brushes another tear away with his thumb, and I sniff. Another tear falls, and he leans in and kisses it away this time, my heart breaking at how sweet and caring he is. But this is Hunter. This is how he's always been, even when we were kids; nothing has changed. It's been hiding underneath for weeks, but I saw it. I knew he was still in there.

"Roman is like a brother to me. Hell, we're blood brothers." He holds up his palm, and I laugh as I hold up mine.

"To say this isn't a strange situation would be a lie." He chuckles and shakes his head. "But it also makes complete sense as well. Which should weird me out. How much we've all been through and the connection we all have together." He smiles and wiggles his brows and I chuckle.

"Mila, I've dreamed about the day I would ask you out, and it might have gone a little different than this."

I pull away to look into his eyes—he's asking me out?

"Oh, sorry, was that *you* asking me out, Mila?" he asks with a huge grin.

Smiling, I let out a giggle. I guess that's what I was trying to do.

"I'm not sure what people are gonna think about

this…but I don't care. Because, at the end of the day, I will have you and I'm all in."

I crush my lips against his and the butterflies are still there. Just like always.

Only, now, they mean so much more…they're a promise.

Of our future.

"We need to find Roman."

FIVE
ROMAN

I hear yelling and sit up, almost forgetting where I am.

The Sons of Death MC has been my sanctuary from the outside world for the past week. I still haven't gotten used to it, all the sounds and partying. Hell, I want this to be my new normal, but I also feel out of place here. Despite it being somewhere I hoped so desperately to fit in.

The room around me lets in light through the thin cream curtains draped over the only window. Duct tape holds it together where the pane of glass is broken. I would say it's been like that for many years.

There isn't much to this room, which houses a man double my age and size. The old mattress I've been sleeping on reminds me that he's lived here a long time. Trucker is exactly as his name suggests—a trucker for the club.

The room isn't much for someone who has lived here for two decades. A wonky chest of drawers, the baby blue paint is scratched and peeling off in places, revealing a neon pink underneath. A green lamp and an ashtray with two thick gold rings inside that somehow don't slide off the other end.

A stack of bike magazines is used as a bedside table where I have left my phone. I haven't charged it or spoken to anyone since I walked out that hospital door. Mila hadn't woken up; she was in a coma when I left, and I couldn't bring myself to see her. I did that—my fucked-up life broke the one good thing I ever wanted.

I'd known that would happen. From the start, I told myself I couldn't have her in my life. I couldn't let the dark that tainted me consume her. But I let her in...just a little. Enough to destroy my heart as I held her broken body in my arms.

The Amarto family hasn't contacted me...but I have to get to them before they find Mila and follow through with more of their threats. She was just a warning, and I heard it loud and clear.

I look at my phone. I really should let Hunter know I'm okay and find out about Mila. I don't want to hear him blame me for what happened. The cops assumed I'd been hit by the same car as Mila. But Hunter knows better. He's too smart and clued in that it had something to do with the assholes at the fight.

There were no witnesses to the accident; the woman who called for help didn't see anything until she heard me screaming out for help. Mila and I were both covered in blood, and it made sense at the time to say I'd been hit by the car. There wasn't another way to explain my injuries and Mila's without drawing suspicion.

When she wakes up and tells everyone what happened, the cops will be after me. I already have a record—just petty shit like getting into fights—but enough that the cops will come sniffing around and that won't bode well for me...or Mila. If the Amarto family thinks I'm talking to cops, who knows what they will do to either of us. Hell, they have cops on the pay. There is no way they would be able to run the way they do without having dirty cops on the books.

The yelling turns into a deep rumbling of men enjoying themselves. Not that I have much to complain about. I've never had a truly good night sleep in my life. I always have one ear and eye open. Waiting for shit to hit the fan. Because it always does.

"Yo, Roman," the voice on the other side of the door calls out before banging twice.

The door protests as it's pushed in. The clubhouse has thin walls and Trucker's room is close to the bar. He's fond of the club bunnies and doesn't like walking far...but at least the guy is safe. His room is littered with empty condom boxes. And that's why I changed the sheets on his bed when I was offered it for the week. Which is now up.

I look from my phone over to Alex. He's wearing faded jeans, a blue tee, and his leather cut. There's a sucker in his mouth, the stick poking out as he grins at me with his perfect white teeth. "How you sleep, Romeo?"

I groan at the name he has always called me. I grew up with him at the trailer park; his parents are deadbeat assholes. He's only a couple of years older than me, but you can see how much that place aged him, like me. Nothing like junkie parents to take any childhood you could hope for. He dropped out his senior year and is a full member of The Sons of Death now. Here, though, he smiles more. Hell, he fits right in, and the MC always takes care of family.

It's what I wanted when I came here, asking Zero for a chance, to be a prospect for the club. I want what Pinkie has. Well, maybe not the name, which makes me smile a little every time someone calls him that. He seems to have accepted it now, two years later. Note to self: don't ever put reds in with your whites or you'll end up with a nickname like Pinkie.

That's why I want him to stop calling me Romeo. I don't want that name to stick. But with a last name like Valentine, I'm fairly certain it's destined to stick.

"I slept like shit, *Pinkie*."

He grins even wider at my use of his club name. "Zero wants to talk to you."

I sit up and shove my feet into my boots that are right beside the bed, ready to go if I need to be fast. I know what this is about. I wish I could just stay here and block out the world, but there isn't room for me here right now. Besides, at my age, I will be classed as a runaway, and they don't need that shit coming around here.

"It will be all good, Roman. Don't stress, man." Pinkie pops the cherry sucker out of his mouth and nods for me to follow him.

Easy for him to say. He has a room here; he isn't sixteen and hiding away from the world in a motor-cycle clubhouse. *Fuck.* I'm not ready to go back to my trailer, my father, and everything else that's out there waiting for me.

"Roman, my boy," Zero greets me.

He's in his sixties, but you wouldn't know it by looking at him. His beard is long and a rich auburn. He has long hair like mine, that's slightly darker than his beard. Not a gray hair in sight, and it makes him look younger than he is. Plus, his old lady is Rina. She's twenty-five and stunning. If Zero wasn't such a chill guy, he would have killed everyone in this club just from staring at her ass. I would have been dead when I walked in here last week. But I think he enjoys the rest of us fools looking at what only he can touch.

"Hey, Zero," I reply. I haven't told him much of what went down. I don't want the club involved in this shit. I got myself into it by having the last name of Valentine. The club doesn't need this on their doorstep.

"Look, boy, I'm not kicking you out. You know I don't wanna send you home to your old man, but he's been asking around for you. And you know it won't be long till he's here, knocking down my door. Maybe bringing the pigs here to get you back."

Zero takes a deep breath as he rubs the back of his neck. The look in his eyes isn't exactly pity, but it's enough to make me feel it.

"I know he uses you to pay for his junk, and I fucking hate the scumbag. If there was another way around this, I would keep you here with me, but we have a lot of heat on us after the shit that went down with Dirty Dan and Itchy over the weekend.

"Kidnapping a minor isn't what I wanna go down for this week. And killing your old man is gonna come back to bite me in the ass, I just know it. But I'm gonna go rough him up and keep him in line."

I nod. I get it. They don't dabble in completely legal ventures here. I knew this when I signed up to prospect. So, I get where they're coming from sending me back. Hell, I would too.

"Look, kid, I'm not kicking you out the club or nothing. You're welcome here any day and time, but I need you to be careful, and if there's any trouble from your old man, you call us. But there is something I want from you."

I nod. Of course. This club is family. Shit, he's gonna ask me to go on a run with Pinkie and the guys. That'll be a step up here. I want that, even though my heart says otherwise.

I haven't been able to prove my worth to the club; they need to know I'm not some liability with a junkie father. Maybe then I will feel like I belong here.

"You seem all healed up after that car accident. I want you to get ready for school. You can take the white Nissan shit-box out back to get you there. Keep it until your bike is back in service. Nutcase is working on it; there's a lot of damage."

I let out a deep sigh. Sometime after dumping me at the cemetery and hitting Mila, the Amarto fuckers took my bike and fucked it something bad.

"All I want is to see a good report card and I'll give it back to you like brand new." He pats me on the back, and I just blink at him. School?

"What?" I stutter out. He wants me to go to school. Right now?

"I've seen you play football, kid. You have what it takes to go all the way. College and shit. I want that for you. No one else had that kind of opportunity here, and I don't want your life wasted here when you can be out there, living it."

I shake my head, and he clamps his hand on my shoulder and nods as he comes in closer. "College," he repeats again, and I just blink at him. He's serious.

"Look, the way I see it. You go to college, get a free ride on a football scholarship, and you play ball and study something boring like business. Fuck, you want to be some arts major, go and paint shit. That's not gonna change a thing here. You'll have a place waiting for you here."

He taps my chest with his index finger and nods again. "You have an opportunity that most people in your situation don't ever get. Take it. Don't waste it, Roman. Make something of yourself. Don't settle for anything less than what you deserve."

I don't deserve anything.

SIX
MILA

Roman's back.

Hunter called me as soon as he turned up at school yesterday begging Coach to let him play in tonight's game. I need to be there; I need to see him. Not that I'm having any luck while I'm a prisoner in my own home. He won't take my calls—it just goes to voicemail. Hell, he's barely speaking to Hunter.

Not being able to see him causes this prickling under my skin, a warning my heart and head are listening to. But there's nothing I can do about it. Even though Hunter said he looked better, I need to see Roman with my own eyes. I won't be able to shake this tight feeling from my chest until I do. The need to see that he's okay is driving me hard.

Coach didn't want him playing in tonight's game. Roman hasn't been at school for almost two weeks, has missed a bunch of schoolwork—not that it seemed to make a difference before—but the excuse of being hit by a car and that he proved he was fit enough to play seemed to be enough to win the coach over.

Last week's shocking loss probably helped push Coach in his decision. Especially with Hunter playing tonight as well. He has his best team on the field tonight, so he must be feeling generous enough to overlook the fact Roman was MIA for almost two weeks.

I know Roman feels responsible for my accident. That's what I'm calling it—my accident. I'm worried Roman is also staying away from me because he thinks I told the cops what really happened. He has to know who hit me; hell, he was hit too…just differently, by the same people, I suspect.

But tell the cops? I would never. It would bring them to Roman's door, and he doesn't need that with the illegal fighting and everything else in his life I don't know about. Whatever Roman is hiding from me and Hunter, the cops would find it.

I haven't spoken to anyone about what really happened. Hunter hasn't directly asked me, but considering the way he talks about that day, I presume he knows there's more to the story. Little things he's said gave it away. Still, the only people who know the full truth are Roman, me, and the two assholes in the car.

"Kate, can't you drive me to the Rebels game? Madison can stay with me, and it will be our little secret," I beg her at the dinner table, my hands clasped together in a pleading gesture.

She eyes the cast on my right wrist. It's covered in drawings—hearts, butterflies, and dicks—that Madison, Hunter, and Asher have done. There's nothing like boys finding empty real estate on my cast and scribbling dumb shit on there. I've had to cover two more dicks with hearts. I'm not the best at drawing with my left hand, so it looks a mess.

I'm downstairs tonight and eating at the dinner table. Thankfully, I've improved enough that I can walk around the house without needing someone with me. I'm sore, and things hurt that I didn't know could from just lying around. But I can't stay up in my bedroom forever.

"Mila, no." Kate shakes her head with a smile. "I'm so excited to see you down here tonight and looking so much better. But I love your father, so please don't use those big blue eyes to ask me to go against his wishes."

I bat my lashes at her, and Madison giggles beside me and joins in. Kate groans and chuckles. "You're both hard to say no to. But *no means no.*"

I let out a long, very audible sigh, and she shakes her head with a grin. At least I don't seem to be getting on her nerves, despite my sulky mood. I've only asked her like ten times to go since she turned up here to feed me an early dinner before going off to watch Asher at a home game. Madison is staying with me overnight. Girls' night.

"We tried. You want to watch a movie now or later?" Madison asks as I twirl the pasta on my fork, using my left hand, and try to shovel it into my mouth without it all falling off. It's weird to use my left hand. But there are lefties out there, like Roman, who use them every day and make it look easy. *It's not.*

I switch the fork to my right hand, and the way the cast and my thumb are, it makes me look like I'm still shoveling. Kate makes a *tsk* sound. She's worried I'll get the creamy pasta sauce under my cast and it will smell. She has a point. I had some M&M's the other night, and one lodged itself just where my palm is, under my cast.

It turns out that, yes, they eventually do melt. And the white edge of my cast now has a brown and blue stain that kind of looks like I wiped my ass with my cast. Okay, so I didn't think that at the time. Asher saw it and asked if I wiped my ass with it. And now that's all I see when I look down at it.

Switching my fork back into my left hand, I put my right arm under the table so I won't be tempted to use it for food.

"I want to watch the game first, if that's okay? We can chill on my bed and watch a movie after I watch the Rebels kick ass. And maybe watch

Hunter's and the guys' tight...ends?" I wink over at Madison.

Madison's cheeks grow red as she giggles, and Kate snorts and chuckles a little, then coughs, trying to hide it.

"Is Hunter your boyfriend now?" Madison asks, and it makes me blush a little.

I shrug and grin widely as she giggles. We never said it exactly like that, but I guess he is.

"Oh my god. He's so cute, Mila," she practically screams from beside me, and I move a few inches away to protect my ears. But I can't wipe the grin from my face because, yeah. He's cute. More than cute.

"He's a real gentleman, that one, Mila." Kate winks at me.

I smirk. He can be a gentleman...some of the time.

set my laptop up just in time for the start of the Rebels game. As I lie down on my left side, Madison comes bearing every type of snack she could find downstairs and some sodas for us each.

"What number is he?" she asks as we both stare at the little red blobs on the screen. I wish I had a huge TV in my room so I could see them all on the big screen.

"Hunter is thirty-three and Roman is eighty-seven."

"Is he okay?" she asks, and the concern in her voice has me turning to her.

"Hunter?"

She shakes her head. "No, Roman. After the car accident? Like, you're here and have a broken wrist and ribs. He's playing football. Did he not get hit as hard?"

Fuck, I hate having to lie about the accident. But I will take the truth to my grave. This time, I really will. I'd told myself I would take the first kisses to my grave, and I told Roman the truth—that he was my first kiss. But, at the time I thought I was dying, and I needed him to know that I wanted him to be my first and my last. I never lied about that, and I knew he wouldn't tell the others. He would take that secret to the grave with him. Just as I will take this one we share as well.

"I was thrown into the air. He tried to save me."

That's exactly what I told the cops, and I won't stray at all from the story. It's close enough to the truth, and it won't change. Everyone will get the same version. That I don't remember anything else, only the sound of the car's brakes, flying in the air, and Roman holding me.

"Oh my god, he tried to save you?" Madison's voice gets higher, and I hear the emotion in her voice.

Her mouth opens wide, and there are tears in her eyes.

My throat grows thick. "He did. He held me...he kissed me right before everything went dark, and I woke up in the hospital days later."

Her hand flew to her mouth. "He kissed you? Oh my god, Mila. That's so much better than any romantic movie or book. He's your knight, and now your boyfriend is his best friend? Roman is just as cute, if not a little scary...*a lot* scary. But he kissed you? Why didn't you ask him to be your boyfriend?"

I look down at the screen and see Hunter. He's standing beside Roman on the field. There's a smile on Hunter's face as he pats Roman's back. I can't see Roman's face, his hair is hanging in the way and I itch to get my hands on it and braid it.

My big Viking. I wish that he'd come to see me. I would have helped him with it. Even if he didn't want to talk, I would've sat here without saying a word and done his hair for him. Just to be in the same space as him...to touch him.

"I'm going to," I reply as my heart aches to reach through the laptop, grab Roman, and hug him. Tell him that I'm here, waiting for him.

"But you're with Hunter now." She gives me a confused look. "Are you going to break up with him already?"

Shaking my head, I smile over at her. I wiggle my

brows, and her mouth pops open, a piece of popcorn falling out onto her lap. I laugh.

"Like, both of them at the same time? Can you do that?" Her brows raise high, and the look on her face almost has me laughing, but I hold it in to save my ribs the pain.

"Yes, as long as everyone is consenting and agrees. Hell, I have no idea how this could work, but Hunter is open to the idea. Roman…I need to talk to him first."

The game starts and she doesn't ask any more questions. I hold my breath as I watch, my heart in my throat as I hope that Roman doesn't get injured. Hunter too, but he wasn't just almost beat to death two weeks ago.

"Next time, we need to watch at my house so we can see all their tight butts on the big TV in the living room."

I laugh at Madison as she stares very closely at my laptop, trying to catch a glimpse of the players' asses.

"Next time, we will see them in person," I promise.

We watch the whole game. The Rebels are so close. We just need a touchdown, and we will win the game. It's been close, which I think surprises most people. The

West Oakley Warriors are nowhere as skilled as the Rebels. But I have a feeling that Roman is more injured than he let the coach know. He fumbled the ball earlier in the game, and the Warriors picked it up and scored a touchdown. But then he got us a touchdown.

"Come on, Roman," I whisper under my breath as he runs down the field. He has this.

I notice Asshole—oops, I mean Jace—watching Roman. Damn him for being a good quarterback. Hunter is running down the field too, and I hold my breath to see which one Jace picks. He has favored Roman most plays tonight. Not that I'm surprised. Jace still hasn't spoken to Hunter, but I bet after he finds out we are together, he will have something to say about that.

Roman's wide open and has a clear run to the end zone, same as Hunter. Holy shit, this is intense. They both have players gaining on them as Jace throws the ball.

I scream as Roman reaches out to catch the ball. He's only a yard from a touchdown, and I know it's in the bag. I scream out in celebration, my ribs protesting. Roman's got it...until he doesn't. He catches the ball, then it just slips from his fingers and bounces off the green grass.

And that's it. The end of the game and the Rebels lost.

I sit there and stare at the screen. There's no way

Roman would have missed that catch under normal circumstances. He could do that with his eyes closed. He must be more injured than anyone thought; he shouldn't have been allowed to play at all. He needs medical attention, not a helmet and gloves. I've been worried all day about this, remembering that feeling in my chest. Roman needed someone to tell him to sit this one out. He'd needed me.

The Warriors are all cheering and celebrating, and the Rebels walk away looking so defeated. A few of the guys are tapping Roman on the shoulder. They must be telling him it's not his fault they lost. Because they, like me, know he's blaming himself for missing that catch.

"I'm sorry, Mila. That's got to be hard on Roman. I know because Asher is the same when he misses. He shouldn't have been allowed to play right after the accident. It's obvious he's injured. He must have broken fingers or something."

I nod. He might have, but he's played with broken fingers before. Hunter told me that Roman plays with broken fingers and ribs all the time. That it's normal for him to have something broken and ignore it. So, whatever this is, it's much worse, and my stomach won't settle at the thought.

When they replay the catch on the screen, they slow it down. I look closely for his injury. But the way his fingers curl around the leather...His eyes, they look down at his hands, like he's just caught a live grenade. It only happens for a split second. His right hand releases the ball just before he can grip it tight, fumbling it, then it drops to the ground and bounces.

The look on his face isn't one I've seen before. He looks at that ball like it wants to kill him, and he can't get away fast enough. It's a strange reaction to have.

I'm not sure anyone else sees what I do; Madison hasn't said anything, but then she doesn't fully get football. And no one gets Roman like I do. Why would he drop that ball when he clearly had it?

Oh god. No…

I freeze, feeling like someone is pressing on my chest and I can't breathe.

Roman lost the game…on purpose.

SEVEN
JACE

t was the perfect throw. How could he fumble that? It fell right into his waiting hands like a baby. All he had to do was cradle it, take a few more steps, and we would be celebrating right now.

But no.

We lost the game because Roman couldn't hold on to the fucking ball. Something a child could do. He came out of nowhere yesterday, begging Coach to play, and Coach agreed to let him suit up for tonight's game.

I'd be lying if I said I wasn't happy at the time. I needed him; there were scouts again out there, watching me, and I had to play well tonight. I needed the boys. But Hunter is a fucking asshole, so I didn't pass to him if I didn't have to, even if the play called for it.

Roman was my choice all night...but that last

catch. I should've known when he fumbled it earlier that he wasn't up to playing. I thought it was a one-off. Apparently not.

It's almost like he wanted to drop it. Like he was trying to get back at me for not coming to see him... or Mila. Hunter didn't play last week because of her. I just couldn't see them. I didn't want to see how bad it really was, so I stayed away. Mom told me how they were. She visited every day.

"Don't worry, Roman. It happens to the best of us," our teammate Zack consoles him as we leave the stadium.

No, it doesn't happen to the best of us. The best of us wouldn't have dropped that catch. But I hold my tongue; I don't want to start shit here. Even though I feel like he did that to punish me. He knew the scouts were out there. The fumble reflects badly on him more than me, but I wanted to win—we all did. Why would he punish the whole team because he's mad at me? The Roman I know would just hit me and get it over with.

Hunter and Roman walk off toward Hunter's Audi, appearing like nothing has changed between them. I guess Roman doesn't care that Hunter has been going to visit Mila every night since she got back from the hospital.

I've seen Hunter over at Mila's, staying till late and shit. I haven't spoken to him at all since Mila and Roman ended up in the hospital. He tried to talk to me, but I didn't care. Fuck him *and* Mila. He made his choice. By choosing her, he fucked this friendship.

This was why we'd always needed the pact. But none of it seems to matter to Hunter. He doesn't care if he loses me or Roman. He wants Mila, and nothing is stopping him.

Only, does she want him? She said we all give her butterflies. Not just Hunter. Fuck it, I don't care. They're perfect for each other. Two assholes in love... Or three.

Fuck them all.

I don't need either of them in my life. She kissed my brother. I hate her. For what she's come back and done, destroying us all. The moment she stood beside her father's truck and waved at me weeks ago, I knew this would happen.

I knew it then, and I know it now.

We're done. What we all once had is gone, and my two best friends have left me. I'm alone. But I'm better off being alone if that's who they choose over me.

"Hey, baby. Good game." Britney slides up to me, and I want to gag at the pet name.

Well, not totally alone.

There's just something about the way Britney says "good game" that has me shaking her off, irritated. But she's all I have now. I might be friends with guys on the team, but Hunter is great friends with every-one. If they take sides, I won't have many standing beside me. Even my own brother would take his side. I know it.

"Baby?"

Fuck, I can't deal with her.

I need Roman on my side. He needs to make a choice, because I can't just wait around with him not talking to me and hope he doesn't fuck me over and take Hunter's side on this. I walk toward where they stand beside Hunter's red Audi and some old white junk car that Roman leans against. Where's his Harley?

They're talking and Roman's shaking his head at something Hunter said.

"She wants to see you," Hunter begs him.

Roman shakes his head again. Maybe I haven't completely lost him. Hunter broke the pact rules, and it's now or never to convince Roman to take my side.

"Hey," I call out. They both turn to me as I throw my bag on the ground and curl my hands into fists.

I'm riled up and brimming with pent-up anger and energy that needs to be released. Hunter's smug face is the place my first hit lands. I don't even realize I've swung at him until his face snaps to the side, and he whirls back, gripping his nose as the blood starts to pour.

"The fuck, Jace?" Roman roars from beside Hunter. He holds Hunter's shoulder and turns him to inspect what I just did to his face.

It has me seeing red. He's already chosen Hunter

over me. Fuck them both. "No, Roman. I should be asking you that question. What the fuck was that shit out there?" I point back to the field.

Roman doesn't speak; he just stands there and stares me down, his chest puffed out, ready for a fight. Normally, I would back down. I've seen Roman in the ring enough times to know I'm no match for him. He has more bulk and muscle on him than I do, and he will win against me any day of the week. No doubt. But I'm also not in the right frame of mind to walk away from this. He fucked up tonight.

I throw my fist at his face, but he grabs my arm, blocking my hit before I can make contact. He pulls me toward him, and I stumble. He takes a cheap kidney shot and I grunt, the pain making my stomach turn.

"Fucker," I hiss out as I stumble back, gripping my side as I look at him.

With his back straight, he's standing tall, ready for me if I go after him again. "Fuck you." He doesn't blink; he just watches me, anticipating my next move.

But I've gained enough brain cells now to know he could have done much worse, and I don't want to end up limping home tonight. Nothing would be more pathetic than that.

"There's no way that wasn't a perfect throw. You fumbled that shit. You dropped it," I scream out at him, and I realize pretty soon that we have an audience as Britney makes a sound behind me with a few players and their girls.

"Go home, Jace. You're angry about the loss and spouting shit." Hunter shakes his head at me. His fingers are covered in bright red as he tries to control the bleeding.

"Fuck you." I point at him, then I point at Roman. "Fuck you too. I'm not talking shit."

Neither of them moves. They just watch me, their expressions unchanged by my words. I'm not hurting them, and they seem to think this is a joke. I'm a joke to them.

"On second thought, the two of you can go fuck Mila. You're dead to me—we're done."

"Jace Montero." I hear the disappointed gasp of my mother. Turning, I see my father beside her, shaking his head as my mom looks between Roman and Hunter.

"Hunter, oh my goodness. Who hit you?"

I grit my teeth as my mother goes to Hunter, and he just stares at me. His eyes never leave mine as my mom tries to get him to sit down so she can take a look at the damage I caused him.

He doesn't tell my mom who hit him, but she puts two and two together as she takes in his nose and my fists.

"You hit Hunter?" She pins me with a look that has my shoulders slumping.

"He broke the pact; he picked Mila over our

friendship. They both did. They don't care about loyalty." I look to my dad for help. He's a guy—he'll understand what I'm talking about.

My dad glances at me briefly before shaking his head and speaking. "I don't know who you are right now, Jace. But no son of mine hurts his friends for being there for one another. Mila was in the hospital, and where were you? You weren't there for her, and now you're breaking Hunter's nose? Why? What does this gain?"

"But Dad..." I start to defend myself, but then I see the figure behind him.

Grady. My brother, my flesh. The asshole who kissed the girl I wanted to marry. That I dreamed of kissing every day for the rest of my life. He knew what he was doing to me when he kissed her. How could he not?

Hunter and Roman weren't the only ones I hadn't spoken to. I haven't spoken to my own brother since I found out. He did this. Started it all and destroyed everything I built.

They all did. They all took her side.

"You couldn't just keep your mouth to yourself. You knew how much she meant to me, how long I'd been in love with her, and you kissed her," I scream at him, my heart beating rapidly. I don't look away from Grady, but he gives me nothing, just like Hunter and Roman.

Britney squeals from behind me. "I didn't kiss

your brother!" I turn to her, her hand on her throat as she looks at me then back at Grady.

"I didn't kiss Grady," she repeats, as if I didn't hear her the first time.

I throw my hands up at her. Why is she even talking right now? "What the fuck are you talking about?"

Her eyes widen and tears track her cheeks. Great, just what I need. *Emotional Britney.*

"Jace. Do not speak to Britney that way," Dad scolds me like I'm five years old again.

I throw my head back and scream at the sky until my throat is raw. I'm so over this shit. Hunter and Roman made their choice. Grady can join them, and they can all fuck Mila together.

"I didn't kiss Grady. I'm not his type."

I let out a deep breath and slowly look down at Britney, who won't shut up. Seriously? What the fuck is she talking about kissing Grady? That's not what I said. Is she not even listening to me?

"Mila. I'm talking about Grady kissing Mila," I scream, my voice hoarse as I watch her expression change, and I suddenly realize the mistake I just made. I did have one person on my side, and I just fucked that up too. Not that I care, I'm better off alone if she is all I have left.

"You're angry at your brother for kissing Mila? The girl who means so much and you love isn't me"

—she points at her chest—"your girlfriend, but the *skank* next door?"

My hands thread through my hair, and I just don't have anything left in me to care. This night has been one big clusterfuck, and I just want it to end. The audience has grown larger, and I know Britney won't come back after this. *Like I care.*

"Don't call her a skank."

I hear Grady defending Mila and, in some ways, I want to as well. But also, fuck Mila. Fuck them all. I snatch up my bag and turn to my dad. I've never seen that look on his face—the one that's directed right at me. *Disappointment.*

Turning to Britney, I find that her mascara has started to run down her face with her tears. Grady just shakes his head at me. But I don't care. I've already hit bottom tonight, might as well make it worth it.

"Britney, I'd like to say it's been fun, but…" I shrug. "I'm a dick. I never said I wasn't. You are the worst girlfriend I ever had, I literally can't stand to be around you."

"Fuck you, Jace. Fuck you and your brother."

I shrug, not giving one shit, and wave my hand at Grady. "Fuck him all you want, *Stink-ney*. We're not together anymore, so you can have him. I'm sure he will fuck you; he likes to take what was once mine."

Her mouth drops open, then she straightens and I

wait for the slap and comeback to that. Hell, I know Grady would touch Britney. She isn't Mila.

"Yeah? That won't happen because Grady's gay."

Everyone grows really quiet; I freeze and slowly spin around on my heel to look at her. What the hell is she going on about? Grady gay? I didn't say that. I said he kissed Mila. Hell, pretty sure half the team who have decided to linger here heard me say that. Britney's gone batshit crazy.

With a smirk on her face, she cocks her hip and points behind me, where Grady stands with Dad.

"Grady is *gay*," she says again, louder now for everyone to hear.

What? No, he's not. I would know if my brother was gay. I turn to Grady, waiting for him to blow up at Britney, but he's standing there, frozen. Staring straight at her, his face has fallen and paled. Dad is grabbing his hand and urging him to go with him. But Grady just stands there and stares at Britney... not speaking a word.

When his eyes meet mine, I can see the unshed tears there. He turns away from me, from the crowd. Dad and Mom follow after him, calling out his name as he begins running.

It's true? I swallow the lump in my throat. Why didn't he tell me? I'm his brother. Why would he kiss Mila if he's gay? So many questions. How did I not know? How did *she* know?

"Britney, you're such a bitch." Hunter shakes his

head. "Jace is an asshole but Grady's never uttered a nasty word about you. And you out him like that?"

His nose has stopped bleeding, but he looks like hell, black eyes starting to form. I almost feel bad for that. *Almost*.

Did Hunter know Grady's gay?

Britney laughs. "I'm only telling the truth, what's the matter with that?"

"Everything, Britney. You just took that from him. You can't out people like that. That's not right," Hunter continues. "I hope you're happy because the team will no longer sit with you. Actually, we no longer acknowledge you exist. You're nobody to us."

Everyone just stares, and there are a few whispers, but that's it. That's when it hits me—everyone here knows Grady's secret. I have no idea how this is going to affect him. She just told everyone his deepest, darkest secret, and I'm speechless. Can't put that back in the box. It's done, and I can't do anything about it.

Emerson walks over and stands beside Hunter and points at Britney. "That goes for your friends too. If anyone associates with Britney Montlake, you're dead to us. Don't talk to us, don't sit with us, and you sure as hell can't party with us."

I look around as all my teammates stand behind Hunter, Emerson, and Roman and glare at Britney, who sputters, unable to find words. Just like me.

This is all my fault, and I need to go home to

Grady. I need to apologize to him. But how can he ever forgive me? He didn't start this—I did. Britney is a bitch and always has been. I should have seen something coming, but I thought, if anything, she would be nasty to Mila. Not Grady.

I walk to my car, my shoulders slumping as I make my way across the lot. How did Britney know Grady was gay and not me...his own brother?

He hooks up with girls at parties. I've seen him. That's the only time he really hooks up. He's at training every day, and he never goes out on dates. Hell, most of us don't, but that doesn't make someone gay. How would I see him with another guy? He's either home or over at Makai's, studying.

Oh my god. I slump into the seat of my car, throwing my head back as I run my hands over my face. How could I have been so blind? I knew having a study session on the first day of school was strange, but I just thought they wanted to get a head start and, I guess, hang out. The whole time, they've been more than friends and hiding it.

I look over to my teammates still standing around, feeling grateful Grady has such amazing friends. Wishing I was an amazing brother and not such a self-centered dick.

Looking into my rearview mirror, I hate the reflection I see. "Jace Montero, you're a fucking asshole."

EIGHT
MILA

Hunter hasn't called me yet. We discussed earlier that I would wait for him to call me because he planned to talk to Roman after the game. To try get him to come see me tomorrow to talk. So, the fact he hasn't called means he must still be working on Roman. He might go to a party tonight if Roman does. Hunter said he will stick with him. Make sure he's all right and doesn't get into any trouble.

Beside me, Madison makes a soft snoring sound, and I smile. She passed out about an hour ago, and I'm still here watching the movie she picked. It's awesome, actually. Miles Teller is in it...and well, anything that guy is in is sure to be awesome. He is cute and so fucking hot. I saw that body of his in the new *Top Gun* trailer. I need to see that movie just to stare at him all day.

I hear yelling outside at the Montero's place. I can tell it's Jace. Great, he's going to wake Madison. What the fuck is his problem now? *The world doesn't revolve around you, asshole.* As much as he seems to think it does.

Carefully extracting myself from under the blankets, I sneak over to my window barefoot to look out and see what the hell is going on. The outside light is on at the back of their house, and Daniel is there, stopping Jace from going farther. I can't understand what Jace is saying until I hear him call out, "Grady, please."

Grady? I look down toward the street and see a dark figure standing there. Did they have another fight? Jace needs to get over the kiss. We weren't dating; he was with Britney still. I'm sure of it. He can hate me forever, but he can't hate his brother. That's his family, and I know they were very close growing up. I don't want to be the reason they have a falling out. But I don't know how to make it better.

The movie playing on my laptop must give off enough light that all three of the Montero men stare up at me. Fuck, I didn't want Jace to know I'd been looking at him. I glance back toward Grady and see he's now gone. Stepping back from my window, I block them out. I don't need to add their drama to my night.

I'm heading back to bed when I hear what sounds like a soft knocking at the front door. Pausing, I listen attentively. Then I hear it again, this time a little louder.

That better not be Jace coming to tell me to stop spying on him from my window. Then I snort. Jace wouldn't be knocking on my door; he wouldn't have the guts to tell me that to my face. The only other person it could be is Grady. Hunter would have called if he was coming, plus Dad gave him a key, so he wouldn't need to knock.

I sneak out of the room and close the door behind me, hoping that Madison doesn't wake from the knocking. The stair squeaks, and I grit my teeth and listen for her to wake. There's no sound, so I continue down the stairs. The knocking starts again.

"I'm coming," I whisper-yell as I switch on the living room light so I don't fall over anything getting to the door.

But as I place my fingers on the lock, I hesitate. What if it isn't Grady and is some crazy killer instead? Like, I know the odds are against this being a killer, especially one who knocks, but that knowledge doesn't help my nerves at all. My hand shakes a little.

"Grady?" I hold my breath, waiting for his response.

"Yeah, can I come in, Mila?"

I let out a ragged breath. I need to stop watching so much true crime. It's messing with my head. Twisting the lock, I open the door. As Grady's figure comes closer, I smile into the darkness. But my smile drops as soon as I get a good look at his face. His eyes are red and glassy, and he's all splotchy and puffy. He's been crying.

"Grady?" I reach out and grab his arm, pulling him into me. Stopping him as he gets just over the threshold, I reach up to cup his cheek. He closes his eyes and presses his face into my hand.

"Oh god, what happened?" I look over his face for any signs he's in physical pain.

He doesn't say anything; he just lets out a loud sob and wraps his arms around me. I feel his body shake as he sobs uncontrollably into my shoulder. It's breaking me to see him like this. I don't think I've ever seen Grady cry in my whole life. I rub his back. I don't know what's happened.

Who hurt him? Jace? God, he needs to get out of his own fucked-up head and think about others around him. What happened to Jace in the last four years that's made him this way?

"Come take a seat. I'll close the door and keep the cold air out." I pull away from him, holding his arms so he knows that I don't want to stop hugging and comforting him.

He looks away from me and sniffs. I see him wipe his cheeks, trying to hide any evidence he'd just been crying on my shoulder. There's nothing wrong with crying. We all have the right to our feelings and emotions, whatever they may be.

I close the door and feel my nipples harden from the chill in the air. I cross my arms over my chest to hide them. I'm not wearing a bra. I was going to sleep after the movie so I got comfy and took off the bra hours ago, like Madison did. We called it "free the boobs" and laughed as we threw them across the room and sighed in relief.

He moves over to the sofa and sits. His hands cover his face as he leans over and drops his head to his lap. I move slowly and sit beside him. Placing my hand tenderly on his back, I start to rub, but he begins sobbing again. I'm not sure if I'm making this better or worse. All I want to do is wrap him up in my arms and protect him from whatever is hurting him.

Grady is a good guy, one of the best out there. He deserves nothing but the best. So, seeing him hurt this much makes my chest hurt. Jace did something. I don't know what, but from the way he was calling out to Grady before with Daniel holding him back, something went down, and Grady is here hurting because of it.

I will go toe-to-toe with Jace. It doesn't matter that I'm shorter, or that I have a cast on my arm, I will hurt him for hurting Grady.

"Do you want to talk to me? Or do you want some water?" He doesn't change position or say anything, so I try again. "Maybe a shot of whiskey?"

He sits up, blinking at me a few times as he gazes

into my eyes. "Your dad has whiskey? I thought he was a beer drinker."

I chuckle. It's true that my dad prefers beer over whiskey. He doesn't drink much, but I've only really seen him drink beer.

"It's kinda old, but isn't that stuff supposed to age anyway? What's a few more years?"

He chuckles and nods.

"Okay, whiskey it is."

I practically jog into the kitchen and open the top cupboard above the fridge, and right at the back is the unopened whiskey bottle. I knew where to find it, since I spotted it a few weeks back when I was looking for a container to make mac and cheese in.

With a jump, I reach my hand up. Fuck, I need a chair. I should have grabbed one when I came in here. Turning, I slam into Grady's hard body. I grab onto him to steady myself as he pulls down the whiskey bottle and gives me a half smile. I let go of him and take it from his hands with a nod and smirk. This will be interesting.

"Yeah, my mom gave this to Dad for his birthday one year. I remember only because Dad said he didn't like whiskey, and I was confused why she would buy him something he doesn't like for his birthday." I shrug. I guess it had been a sign that their marriage wasn't good. Not that I would have realized that then. I'd just been a kid and hadn't known what to look for.

"Two glasses?" he asks, and I wiggle my brows and stick out my tongue. It makes him grin.

"Can't let you drink alone."

We put the whiskey bottle on the coffee table. I'm sure Dad will be okay with us having a little. It was just collecting dust back there, and the last thing he needs is another remind of Mom in this house. Maybe it's best if we don't tell Dad at all. He's pretty cool about stuff, but I'm not sure how cool he is about underage drinking in his house.

There's not a shot glass to be found, so our tall water glasses are all I have to work with. Grady pours a generous amount of the amber liquid into my glass, and when I move to stop him, he just smirks at me as he moves to pour his glass. I shiver at the thought of the taste. Whiskey is not my liquor of choice, and I'm about to break my no drinking rule for it. But for Grady, tonight, I will happily break that rule.

I take a small sip and swallow. "Gah, shit." I open my mouth and stick out my tongue. Fucking gross. How do people drink this shit straight? I release a deep breath, and I feel like I'm breathing fire. That stuff is strong as hell.

I turn to see Grady pouring himself another. He chases it down right after the first and starts pouring another. Fuck, whatever happened must be bad.

"Hey, wait, slow down. Let me catch up." I hold my hand to stop him, and he looks down at my cast.

"Shit, you're supposed to be on bed rest, and I dragged you down here in the middle of the night. I'm so sorry, Mila."

I shake my head. "No, you didn't. I'm not on bed rest anymore, but I'm still on babysitter watch. Got Madison over here."

He looks around, then to the stairs. "Is she upstairs waiting for you?"

"No, she passed out over an hour ago. A fourteen-year-old girl is babysitting me and fell asleep and now I'm getting into trouble with the cute boy next door." I giggle and Grady does too.

It's cute, though. She tried so hard to stay awake, but she said it was a rough two weeks, and I know that's because of me. She needs all the sleep she can get.

I decide to throw back the rest of the whiskey in my glass and get a second with Grady...or is it his third? Wait, is it his fourth? After this one, I'm putting the bottle away. I don't need him going home drunk. Ella and Daniel won't be happy with me if he pukes everywhere. Which I suspect he will, with how much he just drank.

"Cheers," we both say as we clink the glasses together, the amber liquid trying to escape over the rim.

I hold my breath and count to three before I shoot it back. So much whisky. My tongue is on fire, and I stomp my feet as I groan from the burn.

"Fuck...oh, shit. That's nasty." I think I'm dying, but since I haven't eaten in hours, I can also feel the warmth growing. I need to stop now. I can't do another with him or I will be on the floor for the rest of the night, passed out.

"Oh, fuck...are you on any medication from the accident?"

My mouth drops open. I have some pills I take three times a day. I didn't think about it. Shrugging, I say, "I guess we'll discover the effects soon enough."

Grady looks worried. "I'll stay and babysit you... just in case."

I bump my shoulder into his, and he smiles but it's full of concern. Regardless, I'm happy to see him smile. I think it's gonna be me babysitting him.

Although I'm worried about him, I refuse to ask him what's wrong. If he wants to tell me, he can. Otherwise, I'm happy to just sit here and talk and make him smile.

"As long as you don't expect to get paid, you can babysit me all night. I can even get the sofa bed out, and we can watch movies. No more whiskey. But we can snuggle and veg out. What do you think?"

He places his empty glass on the coffee table and sits back, his long arm coming up over the top of the sofa. Lost in thought, he pulls on a loose strand of my hair. My heart starts to race. *What's wrong, Grady? Please tell me.*

"I couldn't think of anywhere else I would rather be than right here with you."

Oh shit. *Shit.*

"Ah, Grady." I tug on his hand and clasp it between both of mine. "It's only new, but I'm dating Hunter."

I thought the kiss in the car between us was just a one-off. That we didn't feel more. Does he? *Shit.* I thought we were friends and nothing more. Especially with Jace and everything there. Oh god, that's why they were fighting just now?

He gives me a tight-lipped smile. I sit up straighter, the alcohol already at work as I feel a little sluggish. Maybe because it's late and I'm tired. Or the medication I have been taking is the type to increase the effects of alcohol. Pain killers don't mix with alcohol. I should have known better.

"I guessed that you were a thing tonight when Jace blew up and punched Hunter in the face and tried to start a fight with Roman."

My mouth drops open. "Jace did what?" I run a hand down my face and shake my head, trying to clear it. Fuck, I shouldn't have drank that second glass of whiskey.

"Then Jace broke up with Britney...I think? I guess. And she retaliated and told everyone I'm gay."

Gay? Did he just say he's gay? My lips are dry, and I lick them as I try to wrap my head around all this. Jace broke up with Britney, and she called Grady gay? I blink a few times and look at Grady. His big brown eyes are practically begging me to hug him and block out the rest of the world for him.

"She told everyone you're gay?"

Grady just nods and gives a small, sad smile. He looks away, like he's worried about what I will say to this news. Fuck, what a bitch. I can't believe Britney told everyone his personal business. She had no right to say that just because she was mad at Jace.

"Grady, look at me. Please." Oh god, my heart is breaking for him right now.

He looks at me, and I see the tears again. I reach out and wipe one away.

"Mila, I'm not gay. But I'm also not *not* gay too. You know? I froze up and ran." He lets out a deep breath, and I feel him relax, like he's relieved to have the weight of his confession off his shoulders.

"You're bisexual?" I ask gently with a small smile.

He shrugs. "I don't know. There's only one guy I've liked enough to try, and I'm not sure if it's just a him thing...or if I like all men and women. You know?"

"I do. And you don't have to label it, Grady. But she shouldn't have done that. Ousted you in front of the guys." Right now, I wish I hadn't drunk so much whiskey, so I could have my head fully screwed on.

Sitting up, I look deep into his dark eyes. I want him to feel my next words.

"I love you for who you are—straight, gay, or bi. It doesn't matter because you will always be my Grady. I'm here for you if you want to talk about anything and everything. Who you like doesn't change how I feel about you as my friend. And it will never change."

I hug him tight, and we settle into the sofa without saying another word. I close my eyes as I listen to the rhythmic beat of his heart. I can feel sleep trying to pull me under, but I have one question. How did Britney know? Unless she saw him with the guy...

"Makai?" I ask.

"Yeah."

I smile into his chest. "He's hot," I whisper, and I feel the rumble of his chuckle in his chest.

"Yeah, he is."

NINE
MILA

I hear the hushed voices of people in my room. The body under me groans a little. Mmm... Hunter. I don't want him to move. I'm so comfy and warm. My throat is dry, and my head aches a little, but overall, I think I just had the best night sleep in ages.

Under me, Hunter twists and shuffles. I hold on to his tee; I'm not giving up the perfect sleeping partner. "Don't move, I'm not ready to get up," I whine. I don't want to move from here. It's so nice, and Hunter is so snuggly.

He stops, and I sigh as I nestle deeper into him. Lips press against my forehead, and I realize pretty fast that they can't belong to the person I'm lying on.

"Madison?" I open my eyes and blink, trying to focus on where I am. Hunter is staring down at me with dark-rimmed glasses and a huge grin on his face. I didn't know if he still wore them, but god, he's *sexy as hell* in them. He smiles down at me like he can read my thoughts, then holds up a mug that smells like coffee. I moan at the scent.

"Good morning to you as well, babe."

My heart explodes at the word babe. He winks, and that's when I notice a dark bruise under his left eye. Shit, I forgot what Grady said last night. Jace punched Hunter in the nose. He sees my gaze is focused there, and he shakes his head just a little to tell me to leave it, then gestures to the mug.

"Oh, yes, please." I need coffee to function right now.

I move a little, and the warm body under me tenses. I quickly turn, and Grady is staring right back at me with a strange expression. The night comes flashing back, and I smile at him. He beams in response. It's not awkward that I fell asleep on him, right? I hope I didn't drool on him.

Hunter moves around the sofa to the coffee table and sits. Holding out the mug to me, he nudges at the two empty glasses and the half-empty bottle of whiskey. Shit, Grady drank a lot more than I realized.

"Well, well, well...what did you two get up to last night?" Hunter chuckles.

Grady makes a pained sound, like he knows exactly what happened with that bottle and now it's thumping in his head.

While Grady helps me extract myself from him, somehow we ended up in a tangle of limbs. It's not weird that Hunter is here and seeing me sleeping on Grady…is it? But Hunter doesn't bat an eye as he hands me the mug and I mumble a thanks. I'm dying, and anything I can do to wake up and function is welcomed.

"You want some coffee?" Hunter asks Grady, and he nods as he grabs his head with a groan.

Madison surprises me next with a big smile and a bottle of water. In her hand, she holds out the medication…the same stuff that I think messed with me last night because of the whiskey. But I don't need the painkiller anymore. I hate the way it makes me feel. I would rather feel some pain than take it. I shake my head, and she takes them back into the kitchen.

"Asher will be here in a minute to pick me up. Mom and your dad are out on a date day. Or something like that." Madison makes a funny face that's a cross between *eww, gross* and *aww, sweet*.

"Good for them. And thanks for last night. I had fun; we should do it again," I let her know, and she looks to Grady and winks over at me. I roll my eyes and laugh. She's probably thinking of our conversation from last night about Roman and Hunter and the whole together thing.

"Madison, meet Grady, Jace's older, nicer, and smarter brother." I wave my hand at him, and he chuckles deeply. I hear the front door open and close. I smile, knowing Asher's here now.

"Grady, meet the amazing Madison. She is sweeter, nicer, and smarter than her brother, Asher." Madison blushes.

"Hey, I heard that, Mila. You wound me," Asher calls out from behind me in a mocking voice.

"I only speak the truth, and you know it." I turn around and find Asher standing with Walker.

He grins over at me. "Hey, pretty lady."

I'd spoken to him on the phone while I was in the hospital, but I haven't seen him since. Hell, I have no idea if they won the game last night or not. We switched to watching movies after the Rebels game and forgot to check. I place my coffee down and make my way around the sofa to Walker. My body is a little sore, but I think more from the way I slept than anything. He opens his arms, and I hug him.

"Hey, no fair," Hunter mock protests as he comes up to me and pokes my nose. "I made coffee and got no hug. He just walks in here, and he gets a hug."

It's true. I didn't give Hunter a hug, and I really want one from him. I remember in that moment that I'm wearing a loose tee and no bra. *Fuck.* Quickly extracting myself from Walker, I wrap my arms over my chest before realizing the best move is to hug Hunter.

As I move in, he wraps me in a warm embrace, and it feels like home. I sigh in his arms. I missed him last night. I hope everything went well with Roman. Pulling my head back, he looks down at me, giving me a quick, chaste kiss.

"Oh, wait up...something happened between you two?" Asher asks, and I turn to see his eyes darting between mine and Hunter's faces.

I wink over at Asher, at first the expression is almost pained but it's replaced with a smile as he wiggles his brows at me. I can't wipe the smile from my face. "Maybe? But first, I need to have a shower, and I need help from my *boyfriend*."

Walker's mouth drops, and he lets out a low whistle.

"Dang, Hunter, you got better game than me. Mila wouldn't give me the time of day. You treat her good, or I will come steal her." Walker points at Hunter and I shake my head. No stealing me from Hunter. He's mine.

"No game needed. She was my first kiss, and she's gonna be my last."

My heart starts pounding at Hunter's words, and I feel light and happy.

I smile, loving this moment so much. Even Madison's standing over by the sofa with her hand on her chest as she watches Hunter and me being all cute and loving. Grady gives me a smile and a small nod. I nod back. I hope I helped him just a little last night. Come Monday, Britney is going to see a new side of me, and it's not going to be pretty.

"Do you need a sponge bath from your sexy boyfriend?" Hunter pulls back to see my face, and I giggle.

I do…very much need a shower. With some help. "Always."

I really do have the best boyfriend. He's a sweetheart and a gentleman, like Kate said. Hunter throws his head back and whoops loudly before gently scooping me up in his arms.

"Boobs! I get to see boobs, so everyone, get out, now," he yells out as he darts for the stairs.

I grin and shake my head. Okay, so, the gentleman part is a little off, as I suspected. *A lot off*. But I don't care. Hunter's perfect for me, and as he takes two stairs at a time, I wave bye to everyone.

Guys are so weird and easily impressed by boobs.

H unter places me on my feet and spins me to face him outside the bathroom. He cups my cheeks in his hands and smiles down at me. His eyes light up as he studies my face before kissing me. His lips are so soft and warm, but he pulls away before we get lost. I pout a little and he kisses my nose.

"Do you hurt at all? Any pain?"

I shake my head, but he raises a brow as if he doesn't fully believe me. I hold up my cast, trying to change the subject of pain. "I have a plastic cover for this, but I could really use some help washing my hair?" It's so hard with one hand, and I feel like I'm doing a bad job.

Kate helped me wash it this week. Yeah, that wasn't awkward at all. Could have been worse. Dad could be single and then I would have had to ask him to help me. Except, no way that would have happened unless it was over the sink.

I would much rather have Hunter help me.

His eyes widen, and he makes a sound in the back of his throat. "Fuck yeah. Are you really sure, though? I can wait outside the door or in your room. We don't need to rush anything; I was just joking about seeing your boobs…a little."

"A little?" I raise my brow at him and smirk. He puts his hands up in defense.

"Okay, okay. I'm a guy, and I wanna see your boobs more than a little." He wiggles his brows and I laugh.

I love how he can make me laugh. I didn't picture him seeing me naked for the first time like this. I would be lying if I didn't feel a little anxious about the thought, but he lightens the mood with his words and facial expressions.

"But I also don't want to rush this. We have all the time in the world. So, if you want me to help you wash your hair, I can do that and not look at your sexy, naked boobs covered in bubbles while doing it."

Boys and boobs. I roll my eyes. "Okay. Just let me pee first, and I will meet you in there."

It's the perfect compromise, because while I do want to show him my boobs and other things, I look like crap under my clothes. I'm bruised from the accident. I know it's nothing to be ashamed of—I was hit by a car—but I don't want him worried about how much pain I'm in when he sees me for the first time.

I want him to look at me with hunger and passion. I want him to grab me and pull me into his body. Kiss me with a deep hunger as I run my hands down his body and into his shorts, rubbing my palm over his hard cock. Him moaning into my mouth as he grinds against me, wanting more...needing more.

Oh fuck. Stop, brain. Go pee.

T he shower is on and the room is steamed up by the time I take care of business and make it back into the bathroom. The plastic cover for my cast is on the sink and Hunter is shirtless. Oh god...I knew he works out and it really shows. His skin's so tight over all those abs. Hell yeah. I won the jackpot of abs and humor with Hunter.

"Aww, no glasses?" I want them back because they make him so extra cute—nerdy hot.

He smirks. "You mean all I had to do to get to see you naked was wear my glasses?"

I chuckle then nod. "Yep." I pop the 'p.'

"Well, I'm glad I wore them instead of my contacts today. I'm a lucky guy; I get to help wash your hair, and I'm not so blind that I can't still see you…see everything." He winks as he grabs the plastic wrap and moves over to put it on. The tee I'm wearing is loose, so it's easy to slip over the cast when I'm ready.

He tries and fails to figure out how to put the plastic wrap over my cast, so I show him and get it all strapped up. Since the shower has been running the whole time, the humidity in the room is thick. But my nipples are hard and needy. Fuck, this is bad.

His breathing changes as my eyes roam over his bare chest. I reach out with my left hand and trace a finger along his collarbone and down between his pecs and over his abs. I get to his loose-fitting shorts and flick the band before dropping my hand and looking back into his eyes.

"I can't wait till I'm all healed," I whisper. I need to say it out loud or I will be tempted to go further, and I know it won't be what I need or want yet.

His pupils are large as his eyes take me in. Nodding at my words, he places his hand over his eyes and turns around. I pull up the sleep tee, but I only get it half over my head before my hair falls everywhere in my face and it gets caught as I try to pull it off my cast. I stumble into Hunter, and when I feel his hands on me, I freeze.

"I'm looking at the ceiling," he whispers, and I let him help me take it off.

Why am I overthinking this? I've never been ashamed of my body before. My chest rises and falls with every breath I take. He stands there, looking up, then he closes his eyes and stands there with his head tilted back.

He's gorgeous and so sweet. This is the boy who gave me his shorts when we had our first kiss because he thought I had my period. Of course, he's sweet. He's one of the rare, good ones, and now he's mine.

The tee drops to the floor, and I look down at it. Then down at the bruises on my skin. The dark patches that feel like they will take forever to heal. Like they will always be there. They hurt to the touch, but I need this. I need him to touch me, to take away the bad memories of these marks and place his kisses there instead.

"Hunter?" I whisper, my body brushing up against his. My nipples drag over his heated skin, and it feels amazing.

His head tilts lower and his eyes slowly open. He doesn't look anywhere but my eyes. My fingers trace up his back, and I pull myself flush against him. I can feel his heart racing alongside mine. His hands snake up into my hair, and he pulls my face closer to his.

"You're beautiful, Mila. Always have been, always will be." He licks his lips, and in a split second, he's on my mouth, devouring my lips as his hand tangles in my hair. The other cups my ass cheek through my shorts and draws me closer to his body. I can feel all of him against me. He's aroused and hard, and it makes me feel the same, knowing I did that to him.

My hand roams as much as it can, but I need to hold on to something, so I grab his ass and pull him into me. The kiss is hot and dizzying. Mixed in with the humidity of the small bathroom, my skin is clammy and warm against his.

"God, Mila. Fuck," he mutters into my hair as he takes a small step back from me, breathing hard. But his hands don't leave me. They hold me like I might disappear.

I lean my body toward him. His eyes don't wander; he grins at me and takes another breath. I smile and tilt my head a little. I know earlier I didn't want him to look...but now I want him to see me. This is Hunter. He won't care what I look like.

"You're breathtaking." His eyes drop as he takes in my bare chest and my sleep shorts, which I need gone like yesterday. But I don't move. I wait for him to say something about the bruises, but the words never come.

My body is humming with need and want. I haven't been able to take care of myself, and I'm wound up tight. I think if he just breathes on me, I will come undone. That's how wound up I have been.

But he surprises me when he pulls his shorts down and drops them to the floor. My mouth drops open at how big and hard he is for me. I lick my lips and reach out to touch him, but he stops me.

"Ignore my cock. We're here to wash your hair, beautiful. Not to touch you or him."

I look at Hunter, and he shrugs as he palms his hard cock against his belly. I'm not sure if it's to hide it from me or because it feels good. But it's not helping me from being drawn to it. He might be a boobs guy, but right now, I'm a Hunter's cock girl.

"You're huge." And that's not a line to make him feel good. He's big.

He chuckles, and it's deep and throaty. "Words every guy wants to hear, babe. But not now. It's hard enough as it is, looking at your gorgeous body and not rubbing one out quickly. It's gonna be hard trying to wash your hair with a hard-on."

I lick my lips and look up to him, laughing. "Yeah, might be *hard* to wash my hair."

He laughs and shakes his head at my silly joke. "You're next." He spins me so I'm facing the shower now. His thumbs tuck into my shorts and panties as he pulls them down, and they drop to the floor.

I step out of them, and we're now both naked. But he can't see me from where he is. He kisses just below my ear, and I feel his body close behind me, close but not touching.

"I want to kiss you, taste you, have you come on my tongue," he whispers, and I gasp.

Who the hell says stuff like that? Holy fuck, I'm wet and so needy. I want that too.

I try to step back to feel him, but he's holding himself away from me. "We're not going to do that now. I'm going to help you wash your hair and not look at the rest of your body out of respect. Then, I will step out and leave while you wash the rest of yourself. And *then*, when you're ready, I'll come dry your hair."

All I can think of is him taking me up against the shower wall and using his tongue on me. My thighs rub together, trying to find some friction. I need to touch myself. But Hunter's true to his word—he helps me in the shower and starts to wet my hair.

I want everything with him and soon.

TEN
HUNTER

I pace in Mila's room. I like the new room—it suits her. They did a great job of putting it together while she was in the hospital. I'd been worried it would be too different; the way the room was before...that had been my childhood. The room as it is now...it's the start of a new beginning. It even still smells like her old room.

Flopping back onto the bed, I dig the heels of my palms into my eyes. Ugh, fuck. I'm an asshole who totally looked after I said I wouldn't. Mila's ass is just as perfect as I thought it would be. But I saw the bruises from the accident, so many of them. You would think that would be enough for the raging hard-on to subside. But no such luck.

My cock is an asshole.

But, to be fair, washing her hair was nice. I've never done that before, and the noises she made went straight to my dick. There was no chance I wouldn't be hard in the shower with her. I think she was toying with me; she kept backing up into me and bumping into me. She would say, "Sorry," but I could hear the smirk in her voice each time. She wasn't sorry.

"I'm ready," she calls out.

I sit up and watch as she comes into her room, a towel around her body and another in her hand that she holds out to me. I pat the side of the bed and reach out and take the towel.

"I've never had my hair washed by a guy before. I love it and want to do it again."

I chuckle. "I haven't done that either. I'm happy to wash your hair all the time…just, next time, you'll be all healed, and you can wash mine too."

She reaches over and runs her hand over my shaved head. It isn't going to be hard to wash my hair. I've been shaving it for a long time now. It's easier to have short hair.

"Bring back the curls, Hunter. I miss them." She runs her finger along the rim of my glasses and smiles. "I love these too," she adds.

I was teased when I had to wear them all the time. That was just after she left for New York. Then I got contacts and barely wore the glasses unless I was at home. I know it doesn't matter what others say, but now it would be different. I'm not the little skinny kid in middle school. I'm a star player for the Rebels.

"I'll wear them around you more." I lean over and kiss her nose. "Now, turn around so I can dry your hair."

I hum a random tune as I dry her hair. She plays on her phone and makes frustrated sounds.

"What is it?" I finally ask. I can't take it anymore.

Her shoulders slump and she lets out a sigh. "Roman. I tried texting him again and nothing. Did you speak to him last night? About me? Us?"

This conversation is one I'd rather not have today, but I knew it would come up sooner or later. Preferably later, as I didn't want to disappoint Mila. I'd been hoping to take her to see Roman at my place so the three of us could talk. Because there really is nothing to tell Mila. I didn't get to speak to him about, well, any of it. I was leading up to it. I didn't want to jump right in.

"Yeah, I tried. Then Jace messed it up by punching me in the nose. Like a dick. Then there was other shit that went down. I left, and Roman followed me back to my place. He didn't want to go home or to a party. But when I woke up this morning, he was already gone. So, I came here."

"We need to go to see him, sooner rather than later. My hair will air-dry. Just let me get dressed and you can drive us there."

I'm not sure if that's the best approach. Roman's always been very clear—he hates us going to his place. But, on the other hand, if Roman is going to listen to anyone, it would be Mila. I watch as she jumps up and starts to pick things out of her closet.

She turns to me and winks. "Meet you downstairs in five?"

I wink. "Sure thing, babe." And I watch as her cheeks heat. I'm never going to stop calling her babe. I love the way her cheeks flush, and she tilts her head just a little, as if she's shy. Mila's not shy, but I like the way I affect her.

Even more, I love the way she affects me. I haven't been this happy in so long. I got the girl—my dream girl.

"Oh, wow, this is my first outing," Mila says as I help her buckle her seat belt.

Her hair is still damp and loose and some strands drop over her face. I lean over and push them behind her ear. She's beautiful and…wait, what did she just say?

"Shit, should we have asked your dad?" I don't want to get off on the wrong foot with James. I've known him for most of my life. He's a really good guy, and he's trusting me to take care of Mila. Hell, he gave me a key to the house, but I can't abuse that privilege or he will take it away.

"Um…" Mila reaches for the ends of her hair and starts to play with it as she worries her lip. I didn't mean to upset her. "No?"

I raise my brows at her. Is that no, as in "no, it's fine" or no, as in "I don't know"?

"Call him." I pull out my phone and hand it to her. He's going to kill me, I just know it.

She laughs and shakes her head. "No, it's fine. I'm with you, and he trusts you."

I give her my best "you better be sure" look, and she chuckles. I quirk one side of my mouth and she shakes her head.

"It's fine, Hunter. *Ugh*."

She better be sure because I don't want him to lose that trust in me. I plan to be in his life forever… after I marry his daughter.

"Okay. Maybe we can grab some stuff from Annie's Diner and take it to Roman. I bet he hasn't eaten lunch yet, and neither have we."

She smiles as she reaches over to touch my thigh. "Sounds perfect, babe."

And I grin.

It doesn't take long before the hand on my thigh starts to tighten, and not in a good way. She's squeezing hard. I pull up to a stop sign a look over at Mila. Her face is pale and her eyes wide. She's breathing fast and shallow. Fuck. What's happening? Is this something from the accident? Like PTSD?

I pull over quickly. "Babe? Mila? Lala?" I reach toward her cheek and she stiffens under my touch. Fuck, what's happening right now? I turn her to me.

Her eyes are facing me, but she's not looking at me. It's like she's stuck in her own head and can't see me.

"Lala, breathe, babe. Breathe with me. In...out... in...out."

She blinks and her eyes roam over mine before she lets out a deep breath and her body sags under my hands.

Fuck, what just happened?

ELEVEN
MILA

Hunter drives by the cemetery and I can't see anything but them...their car...the men from the fight.

"Well, hello there, angel."

My heart races, and all I can see is their twisted faces as they laughed cruelly at me. I feel hands touch my face, and I freeze. I can't breathe, my chest feeling like it's being compressed.

"In...out...in...out," Hunter says in a calming voice. He's here, with me. I'm safe. I blink and see him. It's his hands touching me, and I almost collapse at the sight of him.

"Mila, babe, what just happened? Are you okay?"

My heart's still racing, and I really don't know what to say. So, I swallow the lump and give him a weak smile. "I think being in the car for the first time since I've been home just gave me a mini panic attack…I don't know why," I add so he won't ask any more questions.

But I do know why. I think the cemetery is somewhere I'll be avoiding for a while. It doesn't take long for Hunter to realize what happened. He's smarter than he lets on, always joking around, but he has a serious side too. I know that, but I wish he wouldn't put two and two together, because I don't want him to feel bad. It's not like I'd known that would happen or I would have warned him.

"Fuck, shit. Mila, babe. I shouldn't have gone that way. It was stupid of me not to think that would trigger you. You can talk to me, you know. You can tell me what really happened that day."

I twist my fingers in my lap. If I say it out loud, that's another person who knows the truth. How many is too many for this secret? I want him to know so badly, but I'm scared.

"I know you've told everyone what *happened*, but I know it had something to do with Roman's fight. Roman wasn't there when you called me. You were leaving, then…it happened, and he was there with you. I'm glad he was, but it doesn't add up and I won't push you or you would have told me already, but I know it's connected."

My fingers start to shake, and I hold them tighter. It's true—Roman wasn't there. I was leaving to go to Hunter. He knew that, *shit*.

"Did you tell anyone that?" My chest feels tight again.

Hunter's eyes are on mine, and he shakes his head. I let out a breath and look around us. We are a little farther away from the cemetery now, but the memories of that day still itch at the back of my mind.

If Hunter knows what really happened...will something happen to him? I don't want to take that chance. But I also want to tell him. I want him to know. I hate keeping secrets from him. Not being able to tell him has been eating me up inside. But the prospect of telling him and then something happening to him eats me up just as much.

"I want to protect you from...them. Protect Roman from the same people...and the law." I let out a deep breath. "Whatever you think happened, it's probably right. I just can't say it out loud, okay? I just can't." A tear rolls down my cheek, then another.

He holds my hand, and with the other, he brushes the tears away. I try to smile, but it's hard. Mumbling something under his breath, he shakes his head. He curses a few times, and I tug on his hand.

He looks up at me. "I want to kill them."

I shake my head. "Don't, it's done. Nothing can change it. Let's just go to Annie's, grab the food, and see Roman. I want him to know that I'm okay. That this wasn't his fault. I'm fine."

I'm fine.

Roman has been protecting me from all his shit, hoping that it wouldn't spill over. Protecting the guys before I came back. I'm worried and scared that Roman won't talk to me and shut me out again. He said he didn't want me to get mixed up in his shit, and now…

I'm mixed up.

As we drive closer to where Roman lives, we pass the industrial park, and the air is thick with the smell of chemicals they pump into the air. It burns my eyes, and I close my window to keep it out. The area is rundown. Graffiti covers every inch of real estate. There are houses with boarded-up windows, overgrown yards with rusty tricycles and broken gates.

As we turn into the trailer park, it isn't what I remember from four years ago. It's worse. There's a thin man sitting on a broken lawn chair, smoking and drinking a beer. When he sees me watching, he gives me a toothless grin and I sink down further into Hunter's seat.

"Don't look at them. Roman's already gonna be pissed that I even brought you here. He hates me coming here. He doesn't want anyone to see"—he waves his hand out in front of him, then grips the steering wheel again—"the way he lives."

"It's not his fault he lives here. I would never judge him for this. I wish he would stay with me. At least then I would know he's safe."

"Oh, if he only would. I've asked for him to move in with me so many times; we have heaps of spare rooms. My dad comes home maybe a few times a month if that, and Mom, she wouldn't even notice if Roman moved in. But he won't. He stays here, like he somehow thinks he deserves this shit hole."

My heart breaks for Roman again. He doesn't deserve this, any of it. All the shit he's done just to keep food on the table is nothing a child should ever have to do. I wish so badly I could have been there for him during those four years, when he hardened himself to the world again.

Roman never got a real childhood. Hell, the only person who got the whole nine yards is Jace. His parents were happy—they did all these wonderful family trips together—and sometimes I wish I had that. Mom wasn't around much, and when she was, she was mean. Dad gave me the best childhood he could. I can't complain.

Hunter's parents were together but never happy. When I was around occasionally, they would fight. I used to think it wasn't too bad, that it was normal to get upset sometimes, like I did with the boys. But now, I'm older and understand so much more. I realize they would have been fighting more than only the times I saw; they probably held back when I was there.

"Maybe we should have called him before turning up here," Hunter's voice is laced with concern, bringing me from my thoughts.

"He won't answer my messages or my calls."

"He's not gonna be happy we're here and will maybe lash out. I don't want you to see that. He does that sometimes when I come check on him. Please don't take it personally if he does."

Hunter seems conflicted, like he shouldn't have brought me here and wants to drive me home again. But if we let Roman have his way, he would disappear, try and save us from himself. We can't let him do that. I won't let him, and I will never give up on him.

"Well, next time he can answer my calls or messages. Then I won't come here looking for him. That's if he's even here."

We've pulled up to Roman's trailer. It looks the same, weathered a little more, but the same. His motorcycle isn't out front, and I worry he's not here. I don't want to see his dad at all. The thought of it turns my stomach.

I turn to Hunter. "Okay, maybe call him. I don't think he's here."

Hunter points to a smaller white car and nods. "Yeah, he's here." But he doesn't sound pleased.

Fuck, is Roman going to be that upset with us?

When Hunter doesn't move to get out of his car, I do. Fuck this. Roman can yell at me all he wants. This is what happens if you don't answer my calls or messages.

Hunter moves toward me in the car as I exit, looking up at me with those brown eyes. Like he's pleading for me to get back in. I ignore him and close the door, turning to the door that's separating me from Roman right now. I suck in a breath and walk up the few stairs; they've seen better days, as they groan under my weight. I don't think. I just knock three times and move back down to the ground and wait.

Hunter is closing his car door when the trailer door slams open and I'm staring at the man who shares his DNA with the boy I'm looking for. *Fuck.* Not the Valentine I'd been hoping for. Damon Valentine, he's changed. His face is gaunt and eyes bloodshot, open sores on his face, and I watch as he scratches the track marks on his inner arm. I grit my teeth and hold myself still. I don't want him to know he scares me.

"Well, hello there, sweet thang," he drawls as he rests against the doorframe, the smell of him alone from where I stand enough to make me sick. "You here to sell me some cookies or something a little sweeter?" He winks at me, and I almost vomit in my mouth.

"We're here for Roman." Hunter's voice has a

warning to it as he wraps his arm around my waist and pulls me close to him. The embrace twinges a rib and I cringe a little. I don't miss the look on Damon's face; he saw that.

He chuckles and scratches his junk slowly. Holding vomit back is harder than I thought. Never have I met a viler person than him.

"He owes me rent money. If you give it to me, I'll give you Roman."

My fists ball and I grit my teeth, so I don't say anything to upset him. I know he used to beat Roman. I'm not stupid. But I don't want him to have a reason to try something on him because of me.

But no way should any child owe rent money. I wouldn't trust Damon with money; I know where he's been sticking it. I want to cry, scream, and rip his eyes out. Beat him with the baseball bat I see just inside the door, until he realizes he's a father and starts acting like one.

Not that there's any point. He will never be a real father.

I don't know what he was like before Roman was born. Was he always like this? I can't see Jeanie ever marrying a man like this. She was sweet and pretty. She must have seen something in him...maybe he was a good man once? But then I think back to the first day I met Roman—his bruises—and I want to strangle him again.

"Roman," I scream out at the top of my lungs,

and the edges of my eyes darken as I keel over at the pain in my ribs. *Fuck*. Fuck…how could I forget?

"Shit, Lala." Hunter's voice is pained as he tries to hold me so I don't slump to the ground.

"Mila?" I hear the roar of Roman's voice and a tear pricks my eye. He heard me; he's coming. I'm going to take him away from here. Away from his father.

"The girl defective or something?"

There's a thump and a grunt, but before I can see what causes it, Roman's there, and I try smile up at him. Oh god, Roman.

My tears are now flowing and they both help me to the car. Once I'm back in the front passenger seat, they close the door and I reach for it. Hunter looks down at me and presses the key fob, and I'm trapped. They move around to the other side, and I can see Damon, holding his middle and slumped over in the doorway. Roman must have punched him.

Hunter and Roman are arguing. I can hear their deep voices, but they don't raise them high enough for me to make out any words.

"Hey," I call out, and the two of them bend and look in the window at me. The look Roman gives me sends chills down my spine.

I'm not sure if they are good chills or bad ones.

TWELVE
ROMAN

Mila turns to me as I sit in the back seat of Hunter's Audi. When she opens her mouth, I let out a low warning growl. I'm not ready to talk. She closes it but pins me with her glare. One that tells me she will put up with my shit for now. But soon...she's going to unleash. She wouldn't be Mila if she didn't.

I need time to cool down after they came to my place. Hunter knows how much I hate it; I hate him being near my father. But bringing Mila there? Fuck, what was he thinking? With his dick, obviously. He needs to think with his head and tell her no, be strong about it. Anything could have happened to her.

The trailer park is full of deadbeats, junkies, and I'm sure most of them wouldn't listen to the word no. Hell, even my own flesh and blood looked at her like she's some whore, and that angered me in a way I'd never experienced before. At the sound of her screaming my name, I'd never jumped out of bed so fast. And the pained sound she made right after had me seeing red. I thought my father had hurt her; I wanted to kill him in that moment. He's lucky I only dropped him.

We decided that going to Hunter's place is the best option. His mom is probably drunk, but she's a million times better than dealing with my father. Not that I would have let either one of them into my place with my father there.

We drive up the streets of the wealthy side of Ridgecrest, which is right beside Lakeview, just a little cheaper. Hunter's family is well-off. They have money, but not as much as some of the assholes over in Lakeview with their ridiculous mansions.

Hunter says his house isn't a mansion, but I call it one. There are six bedrooms, a huge staircase, and marble tiles that run throughout the lower level. They live on all this land and have a pool. But Hunter's house isn't a home. It's cold, to the point it doesn't feel lived-in. I prefer Jace's house; it's warm and inviting. Ella is always cooking amazing meals, always asking me to stay for dinner. That won't be happening for a long time now. I'm done with Jace. I hate who he's become.

Hunter's mom's version of cooking is opening takeout containers and saying, "Grab a plate." It's not the same. Although, it's unfair to compare them, considering where I live and that I cook my own food.

When I was younger and I pictured a future for myself, it was always in a house like Jace's...or Mila's. Growing up, that's what I wanted. I told my mom that, one day, we would live next door to Mila. Then Mom died, and I was left with an asshole whose only ambition is to see how many drugs he can take without dying. Days like today, I wish he would just OD and get it over with.

Hunter stops the car; I reach over and grab the food they bought from Annie's Diner and get out. We all walk in silence to the front door, waiting as Hunter unlocks it.

"Mom, I'm home, and I have visitors." The sound of his voice echoes off the walls. We stand still for a moment. I strain my ears to hear her reply, but there's none.

Hunter turns to us and gives us a half smile and shrug. "She must be sleeping. Let's go eat on the back deck."

I don't say anything to that. We both know that it's more likely that she's passed out. With as much as she drinks, she blacks out a lot. And since Hunter's dad is barely around, he has to take care of her. More often than not.

As I follow behind with the food, Mila keeps glancing back at me. Does she think I'm going to run? I would be lying if I said the idea hadn't crossed my mind. Not because I don't want to be with her. Hell, I love this girl. If I could keep her as mine forever, I would.

But too much has gone down for it to be a good idea to spend time with Mila and Hunter here. The Amato family found me right after I left the club on Thursday. Fuckers were waiting for me. They cut me off and wanted to have a word with me.

I lost the game last night to pay off my father's debt. But that won't be the last I see of them. They'll want more, and I know it. That's why I have to stay away.

I haven't been to The Shed since I got out of the hospital. No more fighting for me. I know the Amato family will always be there, and if I don't fight, they'll forget about me soon enough. At least, I hope they will.

Mila needs me to stay away from her. After today, I won't have contact with her any more than necessary. I tried to keep her from everything, but I let myself fall too deep with her. I let her touch me, I touched her, kissed her. Hell, she braided my hair, and it felt so nice, it was easy to forget all the bad shit and let her in again. But after today, I will go back to ignoring her. I can't undo all that's happened so far, but at least I can prevent any more bad shit from touching her.

"Roman?"

I turn to Mila. She holds out her left hand for the bag of food, and for the first time, I see the cast. The sight of it reminds me why I have to stick to my guns. Why I can't keep her, even as a friend. Mila is too beautiful to ever be tainted with the evil that follows me.

I hand it to her and she brushes her thumb over mine. With that small touch, I want to take back all my thoughts of letting her go. I release the bag and take a step away, shaking my hand as if the feeling of her touch will leave faster. These thoughts, that I could actually be more with Mila, almost killed her. I have to remember that.

"Roman? Are you going to sit and eat or stand there all day?" Mila asks in a light, teasing way.

Without a word, I take a seat beside Hunter. He gives me a pointed look; I know I'm being rude. Her hating me is for the best. It will make everything easier.

"Roman, I want to talk to you. About what happened. I want—"

I put my hand up to stop her. "We don't need to talk about it." When she shakes her head, I add, "I don't want to talk about it."

She lets out a huffing sound, and I look over at her. Her eyes narrow in my direction, and her cute little nose is all bunched up. I forget how headstrong she can be sometimes. Which makes this much harder.

"Well, I do. I want to tell you what happened wasn't your fault."

I make a sound in the back of my throat, and she rolls her eyes.

"Just stop it, listen. It wasn't okay. And I didn't tell anyone what really happened." She looks to Hunter and she lowers her eyes.

She didn't even tell Hunter. Why?

"I only want to protect you, Roman. Like you protect me."

"But I didn't," I protest. "I almost got you killed. I broke my rule and let you in and you almost died, Mila. This is why we can't be friends," I yell. I don't mean to, but she needs to understand. This is it. I can't sugarcoat this shit.

Shaking her head, she looks up at the sky. It's so blue, with barely a cloud. She takes a few deep breaths, as though she's searching for the right words. When her head lowers, she looks right at me. "You know I won't give you up. I won't. So, don't push me away. You know that's not gonna happen. I want you, Roman. I want to spend my life with you."

"You have Hunter for that," I point out a little harsher than I intended. I should be happy; she picked the right one.

Hunter is caring and makes her laugh. She needs someone like that, someone who can take care of her and, when things get serious, lighten the mood. I'm the opposite of Hunter. She doesn't need me. I have nothing. I don't understand why she still cares for me. Why she won't just give me up.

"You give me butterflies, Roman. You both do. I don't want to pick one over the other, and Hunter knows this. What we have…it includes you. If you want. I know it's different and not conventional. Then again, who wants to walk with the crowd when the three of us are strong enough to walk against it?"

What is happening? Is she talking about the three of us, together? I shake my head. That's…I have no words for that.

"Walk with us, Roman. Even if it's just in friendship. I want you by my side, always. I never want to lose you again. I won't. I just can't."

I shake my head again. I can't either. I have to protect her.

"Do you care about me, Roman?" she pleads.

There are tears in her eyes, and I force myself to remain strong. I clear my throat and look down at the food. "Mila, you know I care about you. Please don't ask me that." Picking up a fry, I drop it back down again, suddenly not hungry. "We can't be friends. None of us can."

I turn to Hunter. "My dad, his dealers, The Shed, and other stuff…it follows me everywhere I go. I have a record, and I'm failing at school. This is my life, and I don't see it ever changing. It's only going to spill over onto you both. I don't want anything to happen to either of you. This is how much I care; I show it by leaving you both alone so you'll be safe."

"Can I have today?" Mila lets out a small sob as she brushes a tear from her cheek. "Can we pretend that nothing bad has happened or is going to happen and we are all twelve again, just carefree and happy?"

I give her a small smile and nod. I can do that.

Give us this one last day.

THIRTEEN
MILA

Roman is giving us today, which means I have one day to prove to him that leaving us isn't the answer to his problems. That I will fight for him and always be in his corner. I don't give a shit if he says we can't be friends. He doesn't get a choice with me. I won't give him up.

Nothing he's done will scare me away. I don't care if he has a police record; he had to survive on his own all these years, never asking for or accepting help. So what if he's failing at school? I can help him with homework. I can help him pass. His dad's an asshole, we can't change that. But we can all deal with his dad. Roman can stay at my house, my dad will understand.

Roman gives me a look; he knows I'm plotting. I smirk and wink. He pushes his hair behind his ear, and I long to braid it again. But it might be a little hard with the cast on. The blond scruff on Roman's jaw has me itching to touch it. Is it soft? Scratchy? I watch him lick his lips, and I'm drawn to them. If today doesn't end with a kiss from Roman...

"Hey, wait right here. I have an idea." Hunter runs into his garage and emerges with three foam swords, a plastic knight's helmet, and my old tutu from when I was little.

"Oh my god, you kept all this?" I look to Roman's arm, his tattoo. This is perfect. We will show him the best day ever, and he will have no choice but to keep us.

"Yeah, Mom stored it all away the last time we used it. I found it a few weeks back and thought it was too special not to keep. Play one last game?"

Wow, play a game. I haven't done that in such a long time. Hell, I don't remember the last time I played here with the boys. Today, we make new memories, the three of us.

Hunter hands us each a sword and pops the helmet on my head. It's a snug fit, and I chuckle as he steps into my pink tutu. He struggles to get it over his thighs; it's elastic but not made for Hunter's body. Eventually, he manages to get it up over his waist and lets out a loud whoop as he shimmies his hips. It looks absolutely ridiculous on him. It's so small and tight.

I chuckle. "Are you the princess or the knight?" I

ask, cocking my head to the side as he turns in a circle and lowers into an exaggerated curtsy.

"I'm both. Don't you know that princesses can rescue themselves? I learned that from an old friend." He winks over at me, and I smile at that memory. I used to say that every time I played with the boys. Hunter remembered. *Of course he did.*

"Do you want me to knight you?" Roman asks, and I love that he's getting involved. This might seem childish to most, but it's not to me. It's perfect.

"Why, yes, Sir Knight Roman." I get down on one knee, and he taps his sword on one of my shoulders and then the other.

"Rise, Knight Mila and Knight Hunter. We have bad guys to slay."

"I'm after the king." I giggle and slowly jog away. It's not my finest work, but a slow jog is all I have in me. I can hear the boys play fighting as I run around the pool. I stop to watch them, laughing at the way Hunter prances around and smacks his sword against Roman.

"We must protect the king from a rogue knight," Hunter calls out, and Roman makes a trumpet sound as they both turn and point their swords at me. I laugh, my chest hurting but in the best way.

I give up trying to "run" from them and instead turn to fight them.

"Ouch," I cry out as Hunter hits my upper arm.

"Oh shit, did I hurt you, Mila?" Hunter drops his

sword and becomes very serious. I bonk my sword on the top of his head.

"You're dead." I giggle. The look in Hunter's eyes has me very aware of the type of punishment he wants to give me for that trick…and I want that too.

"You walked into that one, Hunter," Roman says as he also bonks Hunter's head with his sword.

I laugh as they turn on each other and dance around, trying to get each other. Every so often, they turn and gently tap me over and over until I put my hands up.

"I surrender. You've gotten better at using swords."

Hunter laughs. "I train with my sword every night…and sometimes in the morning." He winks at me, and my mouth drops open. He didn't just tell us how often he jerks off. Did he?

Roman's shaking his head. "I didn't need to know how often you play with your *dick*."

"But now you know. You're welcome." Hunter does another curtsy, and I just laugh as Roman pushes him over and he rolls onto the grass.

I lower myself to sit on the grass. "You know what's weird?" I start as both the guys look over at me.

"That I always think of you while I jack off?" Hunter smirks at me.

I try to hide my smile. Stupid ass. "No. But we both know not to shake your hand anymore."

Roman gives off a deep chuckle, and I can't wipe the grin from my face. I love that sound.

"It's that one day, we played this game and went home. And that was the last day we did that. Without knowing, it was the last day you played with your friends like that. No more fun with fake swords or dress up tutus. It became all about makeup and football, parties, and drinking. And just like that, no more innocent fun like a sword fight with friends."

There's only silence as we all look at each other, processing my words. Because it's true. Hunter's mom kept these things for next time, only there wasn't a next time. And none of us saw that coming. How could we have known that was the last time?

"This is that moment, right now." Roman is the first to speak. He pulls up some shards of grass and throws them as he looks over at the pool. The sun shining on the blue looks like glitter, so inviting.

"Yeah, this is it," I reply. The fun and laugher are gone. I killed the happy mood.

"Wanna go swimming?" Hunter asks, changing the subject. I give him a puzzled look. "What? You can borrow something to swim in."

That's what he thinks I'm worried about? I hold up my arm, showing him the cast.

His brows raise and he shakes his head. "Oh yeah, I forgot about that. We can wrap it in a plastic bag."

I smile at him. It would be nice to swim before the weather changes and it gets too cold. Today's nice, but storms are expected over the next week. So, it's maybe the last chance I'll have.

"Yeah, okay, go get a bag...and a t-shirt. I'll swim."

Hunter jumps up and runs to his house, leaving me alone with Roman.

Roman reaches over and holds my fingers with his right hand. I hold still, my pulse picking up at the touch. He moves closer and runs the tip of his index finger over my cast. I realize he's looking at the drawings. But I can't think straight, the butterflies in my belly intensifying at his touch. He runs a finger over a few drawings, and I see the smirk on his face when he finds a hidden cock and balls. I designed around them with the intention of blending the vulgar drawing into the surrounding images so you have to really look for it. But teachers won't call me out on it at school.

"Did Hunter draw all these?" he asks.

I snort. "And Asher. The two of them had a dick-drawing competition on my arm. I would have preferred anything but dicks. But boys and their junk." I shrug. Could have been worse, they could have drawn boobs too.

Roman laughs. He actually shows teeth. *Holy shit*. I need to find more things to make him laugh again. I've missed that sound and I want it back.

Hunter comes running back toward us, holding up a black trash bag and a white t-shirt. I shake my head.

"Really? White? You didn't happen to have any other colors?"

He looks to the tee in his hand, and I watch as the light bulb goes off inside his head and he chuckles to himself. "Ah, yeah. Actually, I wasn't thinking. You can have the one I'm wearing now."

Dropping the white one and the trash bag, he takes of his tee in one swift move. Holy shit. That was smooth. No idea why, but that's the sexiest way to take off a t-shirt.

"Okay, both of you turn around, and I will pop this on."

I take off my tee and shorts. My bra and underwear will be fine getting wet since I can dry them in the sun after. Plus, I can always borrow some boxers from Hunter if I need too. But I don't want to give anyone an eyeful, or for Roman to see my bruises. Hence, the tee to cover me and for them to turn around. Hunter's shirt smells just like him, and it's warm. I hug my waist and take a deep breath of his scent. His cologne is yummy.

When I turn around, both of them are facing away from me in their boxers, blue for Hunter and black for Roman. Those are some tight asses. I chuckle to myself.

I spot the fading bruises on Roman's back, but I

don't linger on them too long. If this is truly the last day he will give us, I'm not going to bring up anything about the day of the accident.

"Ready."

They turn. Roman holds out the trash bag, and Hunter grins widely with duct tape. Oh god. Really? I look at my arm and hope it won't rip out hairs. *Or skin.*

"All right, cover me up." I hold my arm out, and they work together to make it secure. I'm still a little worried, but I don't want to miss out on this. This has been a really nice afternoon, and I don't want it to stop.

Hunter is the first to run and dive in. He's gotten much better at that. Roman holds out his hand to me, and I take it with a smile. He leads me around to the stairs, helps me in, and I sit on the first step. I'm a little worried the bag won't hold and I will mess up my cast.

"Just wait there," Roman instructs, and he dashes off to the garage. It doesn't take long before he emerges with a purple pool float lounger. It's all pumped up and ready to go.

He jogs back over and places it in front of me. With Roman holding my hand, I stand, and he helps me on so I don't fall off. I wiggle to sit up, the plastic sticking to my thighs and making horrible sounds as I try to get comfy. I laugh; it sounds like I'm farting. I lie my head back and close my eyes.

"Ready?" Roman asks and I hum. I haven't been in a pool in ages, and I haven't been in this one in four years. I forgot how much I love the water.

He moves the lounger, and my eyes fly open as I grip the edges, worried I'm going to tip over.

"I won't let you fall. Ever. You can trust me, Mila."

I reach out slowly to his face. He watches my hand but doesn't move away, so I push his hair behind his head. "You need a haircut," I tease, thinking back to that day, of our first kiss. And I can see he remembers too.

His eyes grow darker as he looks out over at Hunter, who is messing around with a speaker to get some tunes going. "I don't want to."

Roman's deep voice goes straight to my core. I feel hot and needy. My breathing picks up, and I watch as his eyes lower to my chest as it rises and falls faster.

"Why not?" I whisper, leaning as close as I can to him. He's right there. I could move only a few more inches and my lips would be pressed against his.

"Because you won't push it away anymore."

Our eyes lock, and I can see he's struggling too. I know he doesn't like to be touched but holding back is killing me. I want to touch his lips and kiss him. Hold him close and feel his hard body against mine. God, I want him to be mine. Always.

He's conflicted, but he said he would give us this

one last day. *Kiss me.* Kiss me again, Roman. I lick my lips, my eyes never leaving his as I will him to make the first move.

I reach out to his face, wanting to show him I want this. But his wet hand comes up and grabs my wrist, his eyes still on me, intense and burning though me. His other hand comes over and caresses my face; it's wet and I feel the droplets on my borrowed tee soaking through. He doesn't let go of my wrist. Instead, he tightens his grip a little more in a warning before letting it go.

I understand. No touching.

His thumb brushes over my lower lip and my tongue darts out to lick it. He groans. His eyes glaze over as he moves in, and my heart starts to race as I close my eyes.

"Mila June Hart, get out of that pool at once."

At the sound of my dad's voice, my eyes fly open, and Roman moves away. The lounger rocks as I try hold on, but I'm so startled that I flip it, and the next thing I hear and see is the water around me and the chlorine in my eyes. I hold my breath, but it's too late —I already got a mouthful of pool water.

The oversized tee is heavy in the water as I try to right myself. Four arms grab at me and lift me above the water, and I cough and splutter as I try to wipe the strands of hair from my face.

My dad and Kate are standing on the side of the pool, and Asher's on the other side, laughing his ass off. I glare at him as I try to hide that I swallowed some of the pool water. I hope Hunter doesn't do anything but swim in here.

"What are you doing here?" I ask my dad.

The boys place me on the tiles, and I cough again as Hunter pats my back.

"Hunter told us you were here, and we got you a surprise so I thought we would come surprise you here. I didn't expect you to be in the pool with a cast on, though."

"I was on the lounger, and I have this bag on just in case. I was fine until you startled me."

And Roman...Dad came and ruined that moment for the both of us. Nothing says cool down like your father using your full name as he scolds you for being in a pool.

Dad hands me a towel, and Kate helps me stand, rubbing my hair and arms. I need to lose the t-shirt, but that would be a little awkward with Dad and Kate...and Asher.

We've finally come to an understanding I think. It's been better—not so sexually charged between us anymore. There's a good chance our parents will marry, and then it would be weird. Or awkward if we didn't work out.

"Let's get you changed, hey?" Kate asks as she wraps another towel around my shoulders.

Nodding, I grab my shorts and tee from where I left them. Hunter leads us inside his house to a bathroom where Kate closes the door and smiles down at me.

"I think your dad might have ruined a moment?" She arches her brow.

"Did Madison tell you?" I ask with a giggle, and she nods. "And you don't think it's wrong?"

"Not at all. If I had two handsome guys wanting to date me when I was your age, I would have in a heartbeat. You only live once—take all the chances and live without regret."

It's the best advice, and I plan to follow it.

I'm going to take chances and live without regret.

FOURTEEN
MILA

A brand-new car…well, brand new to me.

Dad surprised me with a car so I can drive to school, and I love it. It's the best surprise. Honestly, I had no idea he was going to do that. I'd been fine getting lifts in the morning, even if it had been earlier than I wanted some days.

That was Saturday, and today is my first day back at Ridgecrest. Even though Dad isn't happy with me and wants me to wait.

"Please, just give it another week," he asks again.

I shake my head as I try to put my hair up in a ponytail, but I give up when it doesn't work. Dad watches me and gives me a sorry smile. He tried to help me with it last week, but it wasn't tight enough and fell out after ten minutes. He tried again before admitting that his hair styling skills are lacking.

"Dad, I'm fine, and I've been cooped up here too long. I need to go back."

If not for my grades, then for my mental health. Being stuck here all day makes me overthink. Everything. And that's not good for someone who got hit by the car of two gangsters. I assume that's what they are. I call them "bad guys," but I assume they're mixed up in all the stuff that goes on at The Shed.

"Call me if you need me. I don't care if it's something *silly*. You call me, and I will come get you."

I smile as I dive in for another hug from Dad. He rubs the middle of my back and lets out a defeated huff.

"You're a stubborn girl." He shakes his head at me as he takes another sip of coffee.

I chuckle and kiss his cheek. "Yeah, but you love me just the way I am," I tease him.

"I'll always love you, even when you're being so stubborn that I want to bundle you in bubble wrap and keep you safe."

I poke my tongue at Dad, loving this banter with him. Looking down at my phone, I realize I don't have much time left before school starts. I give him another huge squeeze, and my ribs feel so much better now, the hug doesn't even hurt.

Grabbing my bag off the table, I dash for the door. "Bye, Dad. See you at dinner. Kate's place?" He nods and just stands there. "Dad, you're late for work. Get a move on." I worry they'll fire him if he keeps spending time away taking care of me.

I run out to my shiny new silver Honda Civic, giddy at the sight of it. When I hear the beep of a car unlocking, I turn to see Jace storming toward his black SUV. He stops for a moment and looks over at me. He pauses, only for a split second, before he yanks opens his door then slams it behind him.

Someone made him an extra bowl of rage cereal this morning. Not my problem anymore. But I linger as he reverses out of the driveway, and the screeching of his tires has me getting into my own car.

Grady must have left early for weight training. I'm so glad I have my own car now. No way I would have asked Jace for a lift. I would rather get hit by a car again than get into a car with that anger directed at me.

Well, maybe not get hit by a car. That hurts. But I would call an Uber or Hunter.

"Mila, babe." Hunter greets me outside of school with a bear hug and lingering kiss that I never want to stop.

Unfortunately, we do have to stop, and when I draw back, he kisses my nose. And, in this moment, it really sinks in—I'm dating Hunter West. My cute best friend who was always scared to use the rope swing at the lake, grew up into this tall, sexy guy who is mine. I stand on my tiptoes and kiss him again, grinning.

"What was that for?" he asks.

"Because you're mine, and I'm never letting you go."

The bell rings and he takes my bag. Instead of walking beside me, he comes up behind me, wrapping his arm around my waist and placing his chin on my shoulder as we walk together as one.

"I'm never letting you go either, Mila. When you said I could keep you, I took it to heart. I've always known you would one day be my girl. I just had to wait until now to claim you."

I turn my head and kiss his cheek.

He gives me a cocky grin as he stands up and waves an arm in the air. "Everyone, listen up. Mila Hart is my girl. Forever and always."

My eyes widen as I take in the students around us that have frozen to listen to Hunter. I grab his arm and pull it down. "I think they know. Let's go before I'm late for my first class because you're marking your territory." I cock a brow at him, and he chuckles.

"Sorry for being so excited to finally be yours that I had to tell everyone."

Well now, how can I worry about being late when he comes back with something like that?

"What class do you have first?" He wraps his arm

around my shoulder as he stands beside me, and I lean into him.

"English with Mrs. Becker. My double trouble class."

"Double trouble?"

I look at his confused face and giggle. "Yeah, Jace and Roman."

"That's funny. What's chem, then? Triple trouble?"

I shake my head. "A nightmare."

He lets out a deep, throaty laugh at that.

Hunter greets people by name as we walk through the halls; he's very popular with all the students. It's actually nice to see. He's nothing like some of the other jocks I've seen. And he makes sure to introduce me as his girlfriend, Mila, but there's no way I can remember all those names.

By the time I've reached my classroom, I feel like I've surpassed my limit of socializing for the day, and first period hasn't started yet. I have no idea how he does that every day. It's torture. Or maybe I'm just not built to be a social butterfly.

Jace is already sitting at a table as I walk into the class. He glares over at Hunter and me. I just raise my brow. If he has something to say, he can say it or fuck off.

Hunter takes my face in his hands and kisses me with those luscious lips of his. I sag against him a little, soaking in all he has to give, and I give it right back to him. A throat clears, and we break apart. I'm a little dazed after that. I didn't see him at all yesterday, but we talked on the phone a bit. He was helping his mom with some stuff.

"If you would like to take a seat, Miss Hart, we can get the class started," my annoyed-sounding teacher says.

I look around for a spare seat, and the only one available is next to the one person who said he can't be my friend anymore. Roman doesn't look at me. He looks out the window as though he'd rather run away than sit next to me.

Deep down, I know that isn't true. And I'm not giving up. He knows this, especially after our almost-kiss in the pool on Saturday. I'm not letting that go...I dreamed about that kiss two nights in a row. I want the real thing now.

Making my way over, I take the seat, and Hunter follows me, dropping my bag on the floor next to my desk. Roman turns and does that head nod hello thing that guys seem to do. Hunter does the same, but no words are exchanged. I'd almost forgotten Roman said he couldn't be friends with either of us.

I need to ask Hunter how he feels. Hell, this is bigger than I thought. Jace is alone because he's an asshole. Hunter's alone because he chose me. Roman's alone because he thinks the distance will protect all of us.

If anything, I've come home after four years to

three best friends and amazing teammates and reduced them to a head nod and completely ignoring each other. I have to fix this.

One of them at a time. Roman first. Jace…well, I need time after what he did to me and to Grady. Maybe with time alone, he'll realize the mistakes he's made. I know we've made some too, but he lashed out at people he cares for, and he needs to work on himself before I can even start to mend this friendship again. That's if he even wants to.

"Hey," I say to Roman, my mind returning to our "one last day" together. I hadn't laughed that much in so long. My stomach muscles actually hurt yesterday from overuse. I want that day again. As much as I love my new car, it's always going to be the car that cockblocked me from what I know would have been an epic kiss with Roman.

When he doesn't reply, I get out my books from my bag. I try to grip my pen in my right hand and the cast makes it too awkward. So, I flip over to my left hand to take notes. I love pen and paper, but I have the laptop too, which will make it much easier to write.

"I'm not giving up," I whisper under my breath, knowing only he can hear me.

He releases a breath. I draw some circles and swirls with my left hand, trying to get used to writing with that hand. I can feel his eyes on me through his hair, and I want to reach out and push it behind his ear so bad.

"You need to," he whispers. It's barely audible, but I hear it.

"You need a haircut." I look over at him under my lashes and catch his striking blue eye through the strands. We just stare at each other, like we're locked in a battle, and the first to blink loses. I won't lose this battle.

"Don't want one."

I still my lips from smiling and swallow, my hands tingling to push the hair away when he doesn't move to do so.

"Why not?" I press on, holding my breath as I wait for him to reply.

"You know why," he mutters under his breath just as he turns to look out the window again.

That's all I need to hear. I sit up straighter and the buzz in my chest makes me smile like the Cheshire cat. He won't cut his hair…for me. He's not giving up on us. Deep down he doesn't want to.

The class passes in a blur, and as soon as the bell rings, Roman is up and out of his chair faster than I am. I race to catch up with him, but instead, I bump into Britney Montlake. Fuck, just my luck on my first day back.

"Watch where you're going, bitch." She shoves me into someone passing by, and I right myself before falling over. Everyone moves away from us, watching and waiting.

"No, you better watch yourself, Britney." I shake my head and *tsk*. "You can do whatever you want to me; I don't give a shit. But you hurt my friend, and I won't stand by and let that happen. What you did on Friday…I'm gonna get you for that, so you better watch your back. I'm gunning for you, bitch."

I'm done with her shit. Hell, her childish bullying tactics were borderline PG. But no one hurts Grady. He's the sweetest and kindest guy. She will pay for that, but not today. I have other things on my mind.

I storm off to chemistry. I know that Britney is in my class, but Roman and Hunter will also be there. Lucky for me, Roman's my partner, which means he has to spend time with me for the whole class. I'm a little sad Hunter's not near us. I would've liked to sit with them both.

Walking into the room, I take my usual spot, Roman swaggers in after me, his books under his arm, and he flips his hair over his head as he pauses to glance at me. How does he just walk into a room and turn me on? I shift in my seat. Gosh, I think I need to set aside some time with my boyfriend to work off some of this built-up sexual tension so I don't jump Roman in the middle of the classroom.

He sits beside me, the chair scraping as he moves closer to the table and places his books down. Does Roman need help in this class to pass? He said he was failing; I don't understand how he can be failing when he needs to pass to play on the football team. I'm just about to ask when Hunter dances into the room and I roll my eyes. That boy is a show pony. He loves the limelight.

"Babe," he says, dancing over to me and giving me a quick kiss on the cheek. "Roman." Hunter moves in to kiss his cheek, and my eyes widen.

But Roman is faster. He grabs Hunter's throat and growls. "No," is all he says, but his meaning is loud and clear. Don't touch him.

"All good, just saying hello to my two favorite people."

"Oh look, just what we need more of—*faggots*," Britney sneers from where she sits, and I see red, my chair flipping as soon as I stand.

I turn to her, and a sound emits from my throat that's half scream, half growl, causing everyone to stare at me. I'm going to rip her eyes out. I reach out to swipe my hand at her, but Hunter grabs me around the waist.

Emerson comes into the classroom right at that moment. He stands there and looks between Hunter holding me back and Britney pretending to study her nails as though nothing is going on. "Fuck," is all he says.

"Babe, calm down. She isn't worth it."

I beg to differ; she needs to tumble down a few pegs and crawl back into the hole she came out of.

"Mila, she's blacklisted," Emerson says. "We don't talk to or associate with her. And you being Hunter's girl…well, you're one of us now. Always have been." He smiles and nods.

Blacklisted? Well, I guess that's a lot of pegs. She thrives on her queen bee status that she's achieved by being Jace's girlfriend and her bullying. That's how she's maintained her reign over all the students. But that status has been stripped from her, and that's much worse than anything I could do to her.

I nod to Emerson, letting all the fight escape me as I lean against Hunter.

He kisses my neck. "That's it, babe. Don't even look at her."

I point at Britney. "Don't ever, *ever*, use that word again. I don't care if you're blacklisted or not, I will fuck you up." I sneer in her direction as Hunter tries to get me back to my seat.

"Mila Hart," a voice booms loudly in the room, and I slowly turn in Hunter's arms.

Mr. Rayne is staring at me as he crooks his finger to come over. *Fuck.*

The principal's office is stuffy and smells like stale coffee. Various plaques hang on the wall from prizes she's won, mostly collecting dust. I sneeze just at the sight.

"Mila, your threat today toward Britney is unacceptable. We don't tolerate bullies here at Ridgecrest. We're an upstanding school, and I have no other choice but to suspend you for two days."

"What?" I screech. "That's not fair. Britney used a homophobic slur against two boys in class. I was only threatening her because she bullied them; any other student would have done the same."

She sits back in her chair and looks out the glass of her door where Britney waits. Hunter and the girl he sits next to in class are there as well.

Mrs. Hadley stands and opens her door. "Ashley," she calls, and the girl gets up.

Hunter looks at me, those big puppy dog eyes switched on. I think he's trying to suck up to the principal. "Is there any way I can help, Mrs. Hadley?" He flashes a toothy grin, and she stumbles a little.

"We're fine, Hunter, but thank you for your concern." She closes the door and straightens out her blue shirt with a hint of a smile on her flushed cheeks.

Hunter…you dirty dog. How many times has he played Mrs. Hadley like that? I need to ask him.

Ashley sits beside me, and as soon as Mrs. Hadley returns to her chair, her demeanor changes. She leans forward on her desk with her hands clasped. "Tell me, Ashley. Did you hear what Britney said before Mila became enraged?"

I grit my teeth and keep quiet. Enraged?

The poor girl goes pale as she looks at me then to one of the dusty plaques behind the principal's head. "Yes," she squeaks out.

Oh gosh, she's so painfully shy. It isn't fair for her to be put on the spot like this. Hell, Britney will probably go after her, blacklisted or not. You can't just switch a bully off like that and expect her not to lash out.

"Can you tell me?" Mrs. Hadley prods.

Ashley nods a little, and I watch as she picks at her short fingernails. I reach over and hold her hand. "It's okay. This is a safe space. Right, Mrs. Hadley?" I look over, and the principal's eyes widen before she nods.

"Yes, it's a safe space, Ashley."

Ashley looks at where my hand holds hers. "She called Roman and Hunter...she called them...f–a–g–g—"

Mrs. Hadley holds her hand up. "That's enough. I have the picture now. You can go and call in Britney."

Poor Ashley. I've never seen someone move so fast.

Britney comes in and closes the door. I don't look over, but I can feel her eyes on me. *Bitch.*

"You look lovely today, Mrs. Hadley."

I snort and then cough to hide it. What a suck-up.

"Britney, your language is unacceptable. You will be punished for your choice of words." *Choice of words, my ass.* They shouldn't have come out of her mouth at all. "But, Mila, two wrongs don't make a right. So, you're not leaving this room unpunished. Instead, maybe it would be better if the two of you served your punishments together. Then we can all learn to get along."

"What?" Britney and I gasp at the same time.

We both look at each other. I want to spit on her—I'm that angry at her. But learn to get along? What is this, kindergarten?

"Yes, tomorrow morning at seven, the two of you will be at school and you will have office duty. That includes cleaning and running errands all day."

I hold up my cast in case she forgot I have a broken arm. Hell, I might as well play the I-have-a-broken-arm card while I have the cast.

"You can still carry notes to classes, Mila. All the heavy lifting will be done by Britney," she adds, who groans in protest. "There will be no complaining. You're both lucky I don't suspend you. Now, get back to class. I have important things to do."

How is it that my first day back at school I'm almost suspended? But what's worse is spending a whole day with Britney. I would rather be suspended, but I know Dad would be upset. I don't want him to have to come down to school to take me home. I will take the punishment for what it is...*torture.*

. . .

The bell rings for lunch and I see purple hair running at me through the crowd.

"Sadie," I call out as this huge, beaming grin approaches. She doesn't stop as wraps her arms around me gently in a hug. I hug her back.

"Oh my god, you didn't tell me you were coming today. I thought you weren't coming back till next week."

I chuckle. If my dad had his way, I wouldn't be here. "I wasn't supposed to, but I'm also not good at staying home. Or following rules, for that matter."

She pulls back and laughs. Her laugh is contagious, and I follow suit.

"Cadence is gonna flip when she sees you're here. You should have messaged me. I would've come pick you up."

I grin. "Got my own set of wheels now."

My bike is probably all mangled. I never asked, but I don't think I want to see what it looks like now. I've come to grips with that day, but I think seeing my bike would set me back ten steps. I have no intentions of riding a bike ever again.

"Are you gonna sit with us at lunch?"

I purse my lips and pretend I'm thinking. "Maybe? Can you sit with me at the football table?"

Her mouth drops open. "So, it's true? I heard about you and Hunter."

I smile. "Yeah, well, it's not too hard to hear when he's shouting it from the halls."

She gasps, her hand flying to her mouth as her brows raise. "He didn't? Did he? Oh god, Cadence is going to flip when she hears it's true."

"What, why? Oohhh…" My cheeks heat as I remember she once asked if I had seen him naked. Now that I've seen the older version, I can say I'm very impressed.

"Please tell me you're blushing because it's so big?"

I smack her arm then loop it with mine. "I will not be discussing my boyfriend's body parts, no matter how big and impressive they are."

Sadie gasps. "I knew it."

I shake my head. "Come on. Let's go get lunch and watch the drama show of the day. Pretty sure there's going to be a lot of crazy." Thankfully, it's not about me.

"Babe, come sit between me and Emerson," Hunter says, a tray of food already waiting for me.

He's such a sweet boyfriend. I kiss his lips as I park myself between the two of them.

Emerson bumps his shoulder with mine. "I like that you and Hunter are together." Then he leans in close. "Was he the real first kiss?" I shove him play-fully and he chuckles. "What? I had to try."

"That's none of your business," I reply with an exaggerated huff.

He looks at Hunter and, with a sly grin, adds, "I guess he wasn't, if you're not telling me."

My mouth drops open, and he points and nods. I roll my eyes at myself more than Emerson. I can't believe I just gave away my poker face like that.

I see the girls slowly approaching us, like they're lambs to a lion's den. Happy for the change of subject, I ask, "Can we make room for my friends Sadie and Cadence?"

A few of the guys look around then nod, and I gesture for the girls to come over. Their eyes almost bug out of their heads as the guys in front of me turn to check them out before shifting over to let them in.

"Thanks," they whisper and look at me, their eyes telling me, "Holy shit."

I have to bite my tongue to stop myself from giggling at them. They are so funny and great friends. I received so many messages and flowers from them both while I was out of action.

"Babe, I got you water, a soda, a wrap with chicken and avocado, a cookie, and a chocolate bar I brought you from home." Hunter points at all the stuff on the tray in front of me.

He brought me chocolate.

"I wish I had a boyfriend that got me food," Cadence mutters to herself.

I feel bad that the girls have to get up and wait in that long-ass line. But they don't seem to be making a move to get any food. Maybe it's the fact that I said they could sit here. Or they don't want to waste any time in line when they could be sitting at the table with some very fine-looking football players.

Grady appears beside Emerson and takes a seat. I smile over at him, and he winks.

"How was the hangover?" I ask him.

He lets out a huff and shakes his head. "I'll never drink whiskey from the back of your dad's cupboard again, Mila."

When he chuckles, a few of the guys and I join in. I'm glad none of the guys are making what came out about Grady on Friday night weird or a big deal. Which reminds me, where's Makai? I guess he doesn't usually sit here. Or maybe it's more? I hope not; I hope Makai is okay. I'm assuming I'm not the only one who put two and two together with them.

Shit, I really hope no one says anything about Makai. It should be his choice and his alone.

Jace comes over with his tray full of food, and the whole table grows silent. I sit on a knife-edge, wondering who's going to break first. There's a seat left next to his brother, but everyone's watching him. What's his move? Since he's standing there uncertainly, he obviously hasn't apologized to Grady. And it's causing tension within the team.

He reaches for the chair just as Britney appears beside him with her tray. "Jace, I've been calling you and trying to talk to you all day. Come and sit with me." Her voice—whiny and desperate—is like nails going down a chalkboard.

Grady tenses and Emerson growls, "Fuck off."

Jace looks around at everyone at the table, and if looks could kill…

I do feel bad for him; the look he's giving everyone is sad. Still, he's the one who dug this hole and is the only one who can dig himself out. And having Britney here with him, that's not going to go down well at all.

He lashes out at people when he's hurt. I get it. I upset him, and he used our childhood walkie-talkies to broadcast her giving him a blowjob. Maybe he thinks I have no right to be upset. But I happen to think that was a low blow, even for him.

I haven't done or said anything to him since. He made his bed. But there must be something more going on with Jace. Either that, or he's simply an asshole. I don't know if there's a cure for that. Time will tell.

They both turn and walk away and the chatter returns to the table. Sadie's expression goes wide across the table, and I nod. *"Yeah, that's what I meant about the drama,"* I say back with my eyes. I see the corner of her lip go up. Yep, this table seems to always have some form of drama.

I notice that Roman is still missing, and I look around for him. Hunter holds my hand and shakes his head a little. "He's hiding from us," is all he says, and I frown.

I wish he didn't have to hide from us. But I know he thinks he's protecting us...I will let him have that.

For now.

FIFTEEN
MILA

"This is bullshit," I mutter under my breath in the school office.

Britney's here, all dressed up in a pantsuit like she's interviewing for some corporate job. As if the office staff will take one look at her and let her return to class because she's overdressed. If anything, she's just going to be uncomfortable.

I'm not dumb, wearing jeans and a thin sweater. It's colder today, and the weather report said there will be storms this morning.

Britney glares at me, her arms crossed over her chest as she taps her toe. She turns back to the office lady with the gray hair and pink neck scarf. "I did nothing wrong; I shouldn't be punished."

Yeah, because she's the one who gave you the punishment, Britney. Dumbass.

"We have a lot of things on the schedule today, girls, so get ready for a busy day."

Just great. I already want this day to be over with. Imagining spending six more hours with Britney makes me want to scream.

"Mrs. Hadley thought it would be good for you two to help out down in the football locker rooms first, washing uniforms and towels." She flips her hand in the air, as if to say, *"That's all."*

I scrunch my nose at the idea of touching other people's gross stuff. Hot, sweaty boys—no, thank you. But also, sexy, sweaty boys—thank you.

"Will the boys be practicing still?" I ask.

The office lady just raises a brow and rolls her eyes. "They are right now. You can make your way down there, and Coach will let you know what you can do."

I have no idea where the locker rooms are from here; this school is insanely big. My last school had the same number of students but half the campus. I have no idea how they even fit that many people after being here and seeing how much bigger the school is.

Britney clearly knows where she's going, so I follow a few steps behind her.

"Stop following me, bitch," she sneers. Her head snaps back and she walks a little faster.

I realize that she's wearing heels; how the fuck does she walk around in them all day?

"I'm not following you. I'm doing what I've been told. Which is the same as you. Or are you that thick?"

Her fists tighten and she stomps a little louder. I can't wipe the grin from my face. I quite like this song and dance with Britney. Can't wait to see what the day brings.

I'm right about the locker room. The funky, musky smell of sweat from all the football players in here has me holding my breath. Music is playing, but when the door bangs shut behind us, it isn't loud enough to hide our entrance, and everyone looks over at the two of us. Great. I hate being the center of attention, and all eyes are on me.

I guess they all know about Hunter and me. He probably came in here telling anyone who would listen about us being together, and that thought puts a smile on my face.

"Hey, Mila," one guy closest to us says as he walks past, wiping his face with a small towel.

Holy hotness. I nod to him. Britney makes a strange sound, and I smile a little bigger.

"Mila," a few guys call out and wave at me.

Britney turns to look at me, like she can't believe they're even talking to me. I wave back to them, and they reward me with big smiles in return.

Jace is here, and he watches me for a split second before turning back to the weights. I glance next to him and see Emerson with a huge goofy grin, waving at me. I chuckle and wave back. He lifts the bottom of his tee and wipes his face. My mouth drops open at the sight of his toned stomach and the trail of dark curls that leads down into his gray shorts. I stop there because I don't want to be caught looking at his junk.

Fuck me. Emerson's fine. I look around for Hunter and Roman, but I can't see either of them.

Emerson comes over and rubs the back of his neck. "Hey, Mila. Hunter and Roman are off with Coach Talon. They'll be back soon."

"Actually, I'm not here for them."

Em raises his brows as he leans against some equipment beside me, looking very casual. But I know it's a strategic move so I can see all of his body and muscles. Not complaining about the view.

"Oh, really? Trouble in paradise already? Do I have to kick Hunter's butt?"

Oh, protective Emerson…he's kinda hot. I cock my hip and place my hand there. Looking up at him, I can see the beads of sweat around his hairline. I watch as one rolls down the side of his cheek. God, that should be a turn off, but it's not.

And that's a bad thing. A very bad thing.

"Could you actually kick his butt?"

The grin he gives me is wicked, and I lick my lips. Fuck, no. Down, horny body. Emerson is just a friend.

"Hunter, any day. Roman…" He leans in closer, and his eyes dart to a door before he looks back at me and winks. "I don't want to die. But, for you, I'll make an exception."

I chuckle and punch his chest playfully, putting some space between us. "No need to die for me today. I'm here because of my punishment. We get to wash uniforms and towels for you sweaty, gross jocks. *Yay.*"

I scrunch up my nose and give a half-assed fist pump. Then I cringe at the thought of all these guys and how many towels there will be. Plus, after they've had their showers…rubbing their junk all over the towels. *Gross.* Am I supposed to just handle them? They better give me gloves.

"Jace," Britney calls out from beside me.

I look over at Jace, who's walking past us now. His jaw ticks at the sound of his name coming out of her mouth. He keeps on walking away, but it doesn't deter her as she chases after him.

Grady walks in with a few other guys from the defensive line. He's drinking a bottle of water, and he makes even that look sexy, his Adam's apple bobbing as he swallows it down. I seriously need help.

Everyone in the room turns to him, their attention putting me on edge. Are they going to turn into assholes? They might have said they're okay with a gay player on their team, but maybe they're not really. I don't think he has corrected what Britney said about him. I heard the rumors all around school yesterday about Grady being gay.

I'm tense as I wait.

Then I realize what's really going on—they're looking at him to see his reaction to Britney being in here. Not only that, but she hasn't seen him, and neither has Jace, as she follows him around like a puppy.

When Grady notices Britney, he freezes. His eyes quickly dart to mine, and I give him a small smile to let him know this wasn't my idea. He smiles back at me. An arm drapes over my shoulder, and I look up to see that Emerson has drawn me closer to him and away from Britney, who has given up on Jace and returned to my side.

As soon as Grady continues on the whole room goes back to normal. Like that weird standoff didn't just happen.

"You smell really nice, Mila." Emerson sniffs against my neck then chuckles.

I push him away. "And you don't," I tease back, just as two arms come around my waist and spin me. I let out a squeal as Hunter quickly kisses me then bends down and gently swings me over his shoulder. I let out a squeak as I try to hold on, but I'm hanging upside down. I'm so glad my ribs have been feeling better because that would have really hurt a couple days ago.

"Are you trying to pick up my woman, Emerson?"

I look up at Em, who winks down at me and puts his hands up in mock defense. "No way. She was trying to pick me up."

My mouth drops open. "Emerson," I scold, but it comes out breathier than I want due to the fact that I'm upside down and trying to hold on.

"See? She's not denying it. Don't leave her unattended in a room full of guys better looking than you." Em flexes his biceps and makes a growling sound.

"Dream on. You know I'm the prettiest, Em. You never stood a chance." Hunter chuckles as he shoves him, and I sway.

Emerson stumbles into another player but corrects himself before pointing at me and then himself and mouthing the word, "Prettiest."

I let out a giggle, and Hunter smacks my ass, the sound reverberating around the concrete room. No doubt everyone saw and heard what he just did.

"You like that?" Hunter rumbles.

I shake my head, but it's a lie. I liked him smacking my ass.

"Hunter, let me down, you big caveman." I pound on his ass to drop me, then I give up as he starts walking through the room.

I let my arms swing while Hunter tells the guys I'm his girl as he passes them. They're all telling him good job, how lucky he is to have me, and there are a few fist bumps and high fives. I just roll my eyes and grin. He finally puts me down on a chair, and I flip my hair back.

His hands rest on either side of me as he leans in, our foreheads touching. The tip of his nose brushes mine, and I see the smile in his eyes, but also heat in there too. I pull on his tee and he stumbles into me, our lips meeting as heat flares all over my body. The kiss is like fire, hot and needy, until someone calls out to "get a room" and we pull apart.

Hunter is just as affected as me. Even more so, I guess, as I look down to the bulge in his shorts. He gives me a wicked grin as he rearranges it. "Are you teasing me so I have to walk around with my cock hard?"

I tap my chin and fake innocence as I look everywhere but at Hunter. But also, maybe I'm worked up and really needed that. He tickles my neck and I giggle.

"Just so you know, you are very lucky to have me, and I'm not teasing…I wish we weren't here. I want to put my hands down your shorts and…" I raise my brow at him and he coughs and straightens up, looks around, then dives back in to kiss me again.

"Hunter." We both freeze and look over. It's Coach Talon, standing with his hands on his hips, and he doesn't look happy right now. "This isn't bring your girlfriend to work day. I told you to hit the weights."

I bite my lip to stop myself from laughing. Hunter's in trouble and has a raging hard-on.

"I didn't bring her, she was already here," Hunter says, straightening up and holding his hands in front of his junk so his coach can't see it.

I raise my hand and the coach looks at me. "I'm here because Mrs. Hadley told me I had to come here and wash uniforms and towels and stuff. I wasn't here to visit Hunter."

He looks to me then back to where Britney's still standing by the door. He takes off his cap and scratches the top of his head before putting it back down and securing it in place.

"Yes, yes. She told me I would have some help this morning. I'll take you both through to the laundry room where you can get started."

Great, can't wait to be stuck in a room that smells like sweaty balls with Britney Montlake. I slowly get to my feet and drag myself behind him, not looking forward to the rest of the morning now after the fun I just had. Hunter smacks my ass, and I jump a little and turn around and point at his shorts.

"Later," I say as I nod at him. And he palms his cock through his shorts. I wink and head to the laundry room.

• • •

The laundry room is smaller than I imagined, and there's not a lot to wash since the person whose job this is has already done most of it. Coach shows us the machines, and we get to work in silence.

The silence is tense...like, way too tense, and I hate it. It feels like the calm before a storm, and I'm watching my back every time Britney moves behind me.

It doesn't take long before the bell rings and Coach Talon rolls some more laundry our way. "Looks great, girls. Just finish this up and you can report back to the office."

I realize he's given us damp towels from the showers. I wait for Britney to make a move and put them in the washer, but she doesn't. She stands against the wall, playing on her phone as if the Coach didn't just come in here.

"A little help?" I point at the towels, and she looks up at me, then to the towels.

"You heard him, finish it up." And, with that, she dismisses me.

My hand grows into a tight fist as I try to hold back my annoyance. It's hard, but I'm trying to not kill her.

The door opens again, and I'm about to tell the coach that she's not helping, but I'm surprised to see it's Jace.

"Jace," Britney purrs.

Ugh, that's more disgusting than these towels.

He looks toward me, and just for a moment, his eyes hold mine. His face is unreadable, but I'm not going to give him any more of my time. I turn my back on him and wheel the dirty towels over to the washer.

"Britney, the office called and said they need you there right now and to let Mila finish off here."

I glance under my lashes as Jace holds the door open for her.

"Oh, wow. That makes sense. I'm not dressed for this dirty work. Walk with me?" She puts her phone away and makes her way over to him, placing a hand on his chest.

He moves swiftly so it drops away. "Coach needs me for something."

I look away from them both and open the washer door, glad that, at least, it will just be me in here with the towels. Even spending time in this smelly locker room is better than being in Britney's presence for another minute.

The door closes behind them, and I let out a breath I didn't realize I was holding. I don't know why I expected him to say something to me.

I guess somewhere deep inside, as much as I dislike him right now, I still long for his attention. He was once my best friend, and it's hard to forget that part of our lives.

I don't hate Jace Montero. It's much worse than that.

I pity him.

SIXTEEN
HUNTER

Friday night football.

Nothing gets the blood pumping like Friday night football. Emerson runs out beside me, all riled up to beat the Port Oak Raiders. The crowd tonight is loud, even though we're playing at Port Oak. The Rebels know when to come out in force.

I see my girl out there with her two friends, Sadie and Cadence. They bring out a side of her that I can't; girl talk is something I'm not good at, and they bring plenty of that to the table. Lunch has definitely been different this week.

Mila waves at me, and I love seeing her wearing my shirt and number. I double tap my chest and send her a kiss. She blows me one back, and I catch it and pretend to put it in my pocket. I can see her beaming smile and that she's giggling with the girls.

Emerson gives me a chest pump, and I shake out my limbs as I bounce on my feet.

"You think one of Mila's friends would wanna hook up with me at the after-party?" Emerson asks as he stretches his legs and looks over to where Mila and the girls are.

I jog in place and look back over there. "Which one?" I don't know them very well, but I could always ask Mila. Or Emerson could suck it up and ask the one he likes to go suck his dick if that's what he wants. I have a feeling, though, that they're not those types of girls.

He winks over at me. "The redhead."

Cadence. From what I do know of her, she speaks her mind. She would probably chew Emerson up and spit him out in a heartbeat if he asked her.

I grin. "Go for it. Cadence *loves* football players. She will eat right out of your hand."

He eyes me warily, and I smirk. Shaking his head, he says, "Fucker, now I'm not gonna go ask her."

"Maybe stick to the cheer squad. At least they'll be at the party. They don't care as long as you have a football jersey on. They will play with your little dick."

"Fuck you, it's not little."

I wiggle my pinkie finger at him and watch as his face grows red. It's so easy to mess with Emerson.

He flips me the bird and runs toward the stands. I see him waving up at Mila and the girls. Hell, maybe he's asking Cadence to the party later. But then I see Mila's smile as she purses her lips and blows him a kiss. All three of them do.

He comes back with a huge, stupid smile. I shove him, and he laughs.

"Oh…I got me a Mila kiss. And Cadence and…fuck, um…"

I cross my arms over my chest; he hasn't a clue what her name is.

"What's the purple-haired one's name?"

I roll my eyes at him. "You're not getting laid tonight." I turn my back on him and jog over to the rest of the team.

haven't spoken to Jace all week. If it isn't part of football, then I ignore him. Roman has been the same, but that's different since he pretty much ignores everyone but Coach. He spent his morning in Coach's office. I tried to overhear what they were talking about, but I couldn't with the music and all the guys talking.

Out on the field, there's nothing but football. All the other shit I leave behind. Jace stands behind the center and looks over at me. I tap my helmet, letting him know I'm ready, and the defense watches me.

"Gold eagle, gold eagle, hut," Jace calls out, and it's on.

I run, darting past the defense. Roman is on the

other side of the field, running, a player gaining on him. I turn to Jace, our eyes lock, and he throws the ball. I reach out and catch it. Cradling the ball in my arm, I hightail it. Fuck yes, my blood is pumping.

A body slams into me, and we go down with a thud. Fucker. I'd had a good thing going.

Emerson helps me up. "You good?" He pats me on the back as I nod and throw the ball to the ref.

"Yeah, I'm good. Let's go."

This time, the play is for Roman, and he takes the pass off and barrels through the whole defensive line, running faster than I've ever seen him run before.

"Run! Run!" I scream as I barrel down the field after him. Ten yards, five yards…touchdown. Fuck yeah! I whoop loudly and rush to him. In the moment, I forget and jump and hug him. Then I quickly drop away from him. Shit…I look to see if he's affected, but he just grins wildly at me.

"Fuck yeah, boys," he calls loudly, then fist pumps me and the guys coming up to celebrate our first touchdown of the game.

If this is how the night is starting, we'll be walking away winners.

And that's exactly what happens. We win against the Raiders by three touchdowns. Roman made most of them tonight. I've never seen him play like that before. Whatever Coach said to him, it seems to have lit a fire under him or something.

"Party time?" Emerson asks as I get off the bus.

"No. Mila promised Asher and Walker that we would go over to their place and party up."

Emerson shakes his head at me. "The fuck? You gonna party with the Kings and not your teammates?"

I pat his back and chuckle.

"You're partying with Kings? What the hell, man?" Beau shoulder-checks me.

"Those rich boys know how to put on a party," I tease back.

Emerson snorts. "Asshole, you know my parties are the best." He shoves me. "Whatever, man, now you're all loved up, it just means more pussy for me at my parties."

I agree; the only pussy I want is Mila's. But even calling it that doesn't sit right with me. Before I can figure out why, Mila comes running out and wraps her arms and legs around my body and kisses me.

"Hey, sexy, I played just for you. I could hear you in the stands."

She gives me a heated look and kisses me again. I spin us slowly in a circle as I kiss her back. Fuck, Mila's pressed against me, and I can feel myself growing hard.

I drop her back to the ground and take her hand.

She looks over my shoulder at Roman. "Roman, you want to come out with us?"

He shakes his head and makes his way to the white car he's been driving while his Harley's in the shop. I haven't a clue how long it's going to take to get it fixed, but he's still driving the crappy car, so the bike must be really fucked up.

"Let's go party with the enemy." I kiss her hair, and she laughs.

"It's not the whole team, silly. Walker's keeping it small."

True to Walker's word, the party is small, and it's mostly couples. The music isn't so loud you can't hear anyone, and the drinking games aren't played with some shit beer. They have the good shit here. Walker's house is easily twice the size of mine. He gave us a room for the night. Since his parents are rarely ever home, he has most of the team parties here.

"Mila, you wanna strip off and get in the hot tub?" Asher calls out to where she stands beside a dark-haired girl. He sways on his feet beside me; his eyes are glassy, and he winks at her.

"The fuck man, that's my girl." I give him a little shove, and he stumbles into a potted plant but rights himself before breaking it.

"I know she is. She's probably gonna be my step-sister when Coach finally asks my mom to marry him. So, fuck you, dude. I was just asking if she wanted to go in the hot tub. She's been in mine the past couple of days. Said it relaxes her body and shit." He shoves me back.

Oh, fuck. How could I forget that? He's right, their parents look very cozy. It's just a matter of time before they get married.

I take another shot and shake my head. Last one. No more, or I'll be wasted like Asher is. And I don't intend on being drunk...I have plans. With Mila.

"Yeah, sorry. The way I heard it...I guess it just didn't sound like a step-brotherly comment." Maybe I'm drunker than I thought. He did say "strip off," I'm sure of it. That's not normal, right?

Walker wraps his arm around my shoulder and sloshes some beer on my feet. Fuck, not on my Jordan 4 Black Cats. This is their first night out. *Fucker*.

"Oh, no. You heard that right. Asher here has a hard-on for Mila something fierce. But don't worry, she cockblocked him straight up. And me."

Don't worry. What. The. Fuck. Asher doesn't even deny it. He's got a stupid grin on his face.

"Fucking stay away from her, Asher," I growl lowly to him. No idea why I'm suddenly so worried that Mila would leave me for him. I've been worked up since the game tonight. Maybe I just need some sleep.

He puts his hands up and sways again. "We do family dinner and shit. It's all good. It's true she cockblocked me from the get go. It's cool with me. The whole Garden of Eden thing, she said."

"The what?"

I watch as Asher stumbles into a chair and drops his red cup and watch as the contents empty onto the ground.

Walker chuckles beside me. "The forbidden fruit. Mila's off-limits, so it makes her more desirable to Asher. He wants her only because he can't have her. You get me?" Walker fills me in, and Asher just shrugs.

Well, fuck. What do I do with that?

ila crooks her finger at me, and I follow her down to the basement. There's a whole gaming room down here, but it's empty of partygoers; the rest of the party's upstairs.

"You beckon, and I come." I smirk as I back her up against the pool table. She squeaks in surprise, and I wink down at her.

Lifting her up, I place her on the edge of the pool table. I cup her face gently and lean into her neck, inhaling. "God, Mila, you smell so good." My tongue traces up the nape of her neck, and I place a kiss just under her ear. Pulling back, I look at her and she chuckles.

"I got the soft and gentle Hunter tonight?" She licks her lips, and I run my thumb over them.

"Well, we've both been drinking, and I don't want to take advantage of my girlfriend. I need to know where your head's at."

"Let's just say, if you needed me to drive home right now, I'm good to go."

I pull my face from hers and look into her eyes. "You haven't been drinking?"

She shakes her head. I thought she had a beer earlier. My mistake. "Well, you can take all the advantage of me you want. I've had a couple, but I'm fine. Not driving fine but fucking fine."

She cracks up with a deep belly laugh. "Fucking fine," she repeats, snorts and giggles erupting. "That's gonna be my new favorite phrase."

I run my hands along the waistband of her jeans, snaking my hands up under her t-shirt. She does the same to me, feeling the hard plains of my abs. I flex a little under her touch and she groans.

"God, you're so hot. Smart and funny. You're the whole package," she purrs.

Mila tips her head back as I run my hand between her breasts. She closes her eyes, and I use it to my advantage. I pull her tee up, exposing her red bra and breasts. I kiss between her cleavage, one on each tit, and place small licks and kisses up the column of her throat, then her chin, until my mouth lands on her lips. She gasps, our mouths against each other, and her tongue dances with mine.

I press my chest against hers, and she lets out a loud moan.

"Get a room," Walker says from behind, startling us both. We pull away just enough so I can see Walker and not expose Mila to him. He's grinning at us. I flip him the bird, and he chuckles. "Or use my pool table. Whatever floats your boat."

Reaching behind me, I grab one of the pool balls. I roll it, and it smacks into a few others.

Mila sighs into my chest. "Getting a room is the best idea."

"Lead the way, babe." I smack her on the ass and she jumps. I watch the glint in her eyes. She likes it when I spank that perfect ass.

Feeling giddy all of a sudden, I flip her over my shoulder and take off running.

Hell yeah. I can't wait to taste Mila.

SEVENTEEN
MILA

We stumble into the room, giggling at the sounds coming from the room Asher's in. He must have found a girl to take to bed with him…and she is moaning like a porn champion.

Closing the bedroom door, I turn to Hunter. "Oh yeah, oh yeah, *oh yeah*," I mimic, then burst out laughing.

"Yeah, that's it, yeah, ride me," Hunter says, mocking Asher's voice. Then he shakes his head. "I can't tease the guy. He was drunk and stumbling when I left with you. Surprised he could get up the stairs, let alone get his dick up."

"Maybe it's not Asher?" But it's the room he's in for the night. I hope he's not drunk enough to forget to use a condom.

But I don't want to think about Asher—I have other plans for this room. It's gorgeous, with a king-size bed and an ensuite that has a free-standing bathtub made for me. I wonder if Walker would let me move in.

Hunter presses against my back, his hand snaking under my arm and up between my chest as he takes my throat. I drop my head back on his shoulder, and he kisses me upside down.

Though it's a tender kiss, there's a possession to it I love. I give myself over to him, and within a split second, Hunter has me spinning. Cupping my jaw, his mouth descends on mine, his tongue finding mine as I grip onto his arms, trying to steady myself from the dizzying kiss.

I moan, and he wraps his free hand around my loose hair, pulling me into his hard body while I snake my hands down his back. We're breathing heavily as I open my eyes just enough to see the hunger in his gaze.

Gone is the funny and sweet Hunter. In his place is lusty, needy Hunter, and I'm dying to see more of him. He pulls my hair back as I arch my chest into him. He growls just under my ear as he licks the line of my throat. Inhaling my earlobe into his mouth, he sucks on it before letting it go with a little nip, and I feel it deep within me.

He pushes me onto the soft bed and walks back a

few paces. Studying me, he brushes his thumb over his lips as he cocks his hip. I feel it all over.

"Fuck, Mila. You're perfect and all mine."

My body hums at his approval. Reaching behind his head, he grabs his tee, and it's off in one swift move. He gives me a wicked grin, and I grin the same as I remove my top. Fuck, I'm so wet right now; my panties are drenched. I need him, licking me, touching me…*in me.*

He palms his cock through his jeans, and I lick my lips. I reach out to him, and when he doesn't come closer, I pout.

He cocks his head. "Needy, are we?"

I run my hands over my breasts, my bra…I need it gone. When I sit up to undo it, he's on me in a second.

"Mine." His voice is low and throaty in my ear as he flicks the clasp and tears it off. He presses his hand on my sternum and pins me on the soft bedding.

My nipples ache for him. I reach up to touch one, and he slaps my hand away. "Mine," he says again as he moves to one, sucking it deep into his mouth and letting it go with a pop. Then he repeats the same with the other.

He grips my breasts in his hands; they're more than a handful for me, but they fit perfectly in Hunter's. "Your tits are fucking perfect, Mila. Everything about you is."

I press myself into him and try to reach for his button and fly, wanting to touch his cock. Wanting to taste him on my tongue. Wanting him to cry and beg out for me to suck him deep.

When he backs off me and shakes his head, a strangled sound rips from my throat.

"My turn first." He grabs my jean shorts and holds his hand above the first button. I look up and see him silently asking for permission to take them off. I nod and help him shimmy them off.

My panties are next, and when he asks for permission again, I nod. This time, though, he rubs his fingers down through the damp fabric and smiles up at me. "You're so wet for me, Mila."

Then he takes my panties, and I'm left bare before him. Feeling vulnerable under his gaze, I twist my body. But Hunter tugs my legs, and I rest up on my elbows as I open them a little wider, exposing myself to him.

A deep rumble sounds in his chest, and his eyes are heated, clearly just as turned on as I am. The way he looks at me makes me feel sexy and wanted.

He surprises me by grabbing my thighs and tugging me toward him. As he presses his body weight against mine, claiming my mouth again, I love the feel of being under him. His hand snaking down between us, he finds my clit, and I almost buck off the bed. I'm so sensitive to his touch, it's crazy.

"Mmm…you like that?" he asks, slowing down.

I nod, speechless as the pressure rises within me. Dipping down lower, he presses his finger into me. I'm so wet. When he adds a second finger, pleasure rolls through me. He flattens his thumb over my clit as his fingers find my G-spot, and I'm in heaven. I hold on to his biceps to keep myself from levitating off the bed.

"I'm close," I warn him. He said he wanted to taste me, and I still want that.

Hunter grips my shoulder as he starts moving his face down my body until he's at my belly. Looking up at me with a smirk, he takes his fingers out and puts them into his mouth and moans. "So worth the wait," he says with a smirk, and I throw my head back.

His tongue finds my clit, and as he swirls it around, I buck off the bed. He doesn't let up, holding me as still as he can while he sucks my clit into his mouth. I melt into a puddle of bliss. My hands reach for something to hold on to as I crest over the edge. My orgasm slams into me like a freight train, fast and hard, and still, he doesn't let up. He teases each and every moan from me until I have nothing left but a hoarse throat, and I sink into the soft bedding.

When he kisses me slowly, I taste myself on his mouth. It doesn't matter that I just came; I need more. I pull at him, flipping him onto the bed. As I reach for his jeans, he throws his hands behind his head and winks.

"My turn," I say.

His button and fly undone, I push his jeans down with his boxers, and he lifts himself so I can take them off. His erection, caught between the fabric, finally springs free and slaps his stomach. Hunter chuckles.

I take his silky cock into my left hand. With a cast on my right hand, I'm not sure I can do this as well as I want, but I will manage. As I slowly stroke his hard length, Hunter moans my name, jerking into my fist. I start to stroke faster, twisting my fist on the up motion and moving back to the base. His eyes are on mine, and his once easygoing position has changed to gripping the sheets and rushing after his own orgasm.

I love this. The feeling I get from watching him come undone is glorious.

He bucks a few more times before reaching for my wrist to stop me. "Fuck, your hand is magic, but I need to stop or I'm gonna come."

I smile playfully…my handwriting might be terrible, but my stroke work is on point. And I don't want to stop. Bending down, I lick the head of his cock. He watches as I taste the salty pre-cum and moan with his cock in my mouth while I suck it in as deep as I can.

"Mila, babe. As much as I want to come in your mouth, I…want…*ugh, fuck*."

I suck harder and twist my mouth, and I'm rewarded with his body bowing toward me, his fingers gripping my hair as he grunts out his release. I swallow down as much as I can before pulling free.

His eyes are glazed over, and when I smirk, he shakes his head then groans, throwing his head back and running his hands over his face.

"Babe." Hunter smiles and reaches for me, pulling me onto his chest, his cock still hard between us. "That wasn't what I had in mind when we walked in here." He rubs my arm, and I pout up at him. He kisses my forehead and chuckles. "I'm not complaining at all, babe. Fuck, if any guy ever complained about getting head like that from the girl he loves…fuck, he'd need to get his head checked.

"I just was thinking this could have gone a little…*longer*. But your mouth is wicked, in all the best ways. That's the fastest I've ever come. It took me by surprise."

I giggle, and he tilts my mouth up to his, his big brown eyes on mine. I love the way he looks at me, like he can see all my deep, dark secrets while promising to keep them too.

"I love you, Mila Hart. Always have, always will. I'm yours."

My heart races at the words. He's never said that

before. No one has ever said that to me. My breath hitches as I pull his face to mine and kiss him softly. I draw away, tracing his lips with my thumb, and look into his eyes.

"I love you, Hunter West. Always have and always will."

Hunter's the first to hear those words from me, and I thought it would be hard to tell him that, but it's perfect. It's everything I wanted it to be.

He rolls his hips, and his cock is hard against my thigh. The height thing is kinda funny. I like it, though. I reach down and stroke him as his hands cup my ass, trying to gain more friction.

"You have a condom?" I ask him.

Nodding, he reaches for his jeans which lay precariously on the edge of the bed. We don't have to move as he reaches for the little foil wrapper and puts it on.

He pushes my hair behind my ear and, in that moment, I wish I had a hair tie. I want to watch everything between us.

"I love you." He kisses me, and I slide my leg over and straddle him.

Reaching between us, I position him at my entrance and sink down onto his thick cock. *Fuck.* I arch my back and break free from the kiss as I gasp at the feel of him seated in me. I place both my hands on his chest, and the cast makes it harder but he holds me steady as I rock on his cock.

His warm fingers skate up my skin, leaving traces of pleasure in their wake as he cups my breast and rolls my nipple between his finger and thumb. I moan as I rise then sink slowly. This is making love. Slow and steady. This is how I always imagined it would be.

My body is waking up again, my orgasm waiting for me on the other side, but slow is not what my body needs. I can't finish with slow.

Faster. Harder...just *more*.

"I need more, Hunter," I tell him, hoping he feels the same. This slow build will take me all night, and I'll still feel like I'm trying to find the end of a rainbow. I love the chase, but I want that gold now.

"What do you need? You like it harder?"

I moan and nod.

He wraps his hand in my hair and pulls me close to his mouth. He growls into my ear, "You want me to fuck you hard? I can do that. Faster? I can make you scream my name so loud the whole house will know your pussy is wrapped around my cock. I can spank your ass and play with your clit, then watch you fall over the edge...over and over until you're satisfied. And only then will I stop."

His palm cracks against my ass cheek, and I buck into him, his thumb finding my clit, and I cry out. And he said my mouth is wicked. Hunter can make me come just from words alone. Damn his dirty talk. Hunter is going to kill me in all the best ways.

"Fuck, yes. Fuck me, Hunter." I don't care who hears me. I need everything, and I need it now.

He grabs my hips, and we gain a steady rhythm, but it's still not enough. Just as I'm about to ask, he flips us and he's pushing my leg up beside my head and thrusting in deeply. I moan and reach for him as he starts to gain speed, thrusting over and over, bringing me closer to my climax.

"Fuck," is all I manage to get out as my body spirals toward that goal. But before I can get there, he pulls out and flips me onto my stomach. "I was almost there," I whine.

He chuckles and slaps my ass twice in quick succession. It doesn't hurt; it's just enough to sting, and it has me growing wetter.

Pulling on my hips until my ass is up higher, he presses on my back, my chest rubbing against the soft sheets as he enters me from behind. He's slow, inch by inch, then he slams into me, and I call out again.

It doesn't take long in this position. I scream out his name as he thrusts faster and wilder, my orgasm rolling over my body as I call out his name. I feel like that's all I have. He pinches my clit, and I moan deeply into the sheets.

"I can't hear you," he growls from behind me, and I turn back, giving him a lazy smile. He slaps my ass and I jerk. He chuckles. "Guess I will have to do that one again."

If that's a challenge, I'm only too willing to accept it.

Long strokes, faster, slower—the pattern isn't one I can anticipate, and I love it. I feel his cock swell as his movements become jerky.

"Mila," he roars. His cock throbs inside me as he spills over the edge. My core clenches around him, and I'm right there with him, gasping for breath as my body trembles from another powerful orgasm. Hunter lets out a whole-body shiver and groans as he thrusts one last time.

He kisses my spine, and when I turn to face him, he kisses the corner of my mouth before pulling away.

He jumps up and into the bathroom to dispose of the condom. I hear the water running, but it's just too much right now. I've had a long day, and tonight... well, tonight has been the best workout of my life.

I'm closing my eyes when I feel Hunter rolling my body and pressing a warm cloth between my legs. Cleaning me up.

I smile lazily at him as he hands me another warm washcloth. "For your face. Sometimes, it feels nice to fall asleep with a clean face."

And that's true. I have makeup on, but I sleep without it. I make quick work of it, hoping I don't look like a panda, but even if I do, Hunter doesn't say anything. He just smiles and kisses me before taking the wet cloths and turning out the light.

Returning to bed, he pulls the covers over us and we snuggle under them. He wraps his arm around me, and I rest my head on his chest, listening to his steady heartbeat as it sends me off to sleep.

EIGHTEEN
MILA

A throat clears. "Mila."

I blink a few times before groaning at the sunlight streaming in the window. Shutting my eyes, I quickly bury my nose into Hunter's throat and groan at how tired I am.

"I don't wanna get up," I whine, and he pulls me in tighter and mumbles something.

There's the buzzing of an alarm, and Hunter rolls to turn it off, taking his body warmth with him.

Why does he have to train so early...or watch tapes or whatever they do on Saturday mornings? It's too early. Why didn't we close the curtains last night? I swear they were closed when we got in here.

A throat clears again, and I hear my name.

"Mmm...babe." Hunter nuzzles into my throat and smiles lazily. I'm a little sore all over from the fun we had last night. "You smell so good. I need to taste you again so I don't convince myself I'm dreaming right now." He runs his fingers down my belly and between my legs, stroking over my clit.

I moan. "Mmm...yes." I want that too.

Hearing a sound on the other side of the room, we both sit up. I blink as I rub my eyes and see Asher sitting on a dresser on the opposite side of the room. *The hell?*

"What the fuck, Asher? Get out," Hunter screams at him.

Asher jumps down as I scramble to cover my naked body with the sheet. Hunter's not helping as he shuffles to the side of the bed.

Asher holds his hands up in mock defense and chuckles. "To be fair, I knocked a bunch of times. I tried to get Mila to wake up, but she seems to sleep like the dead. And you snore, Hunter."

Hunter snores? Why would Asher be waking me...*Oh, fuck.* He's supposed to give me a ride to his house. No, I'm giving him one. Since he wanted to drink, he got a lift here, and I promised to take him home so he could ride to training with Dad. I forgot.

"Shit, I'm supposed to drive Asher home."

But that doesn't seem to placate my boyfriend. Hunter's worked up as he stands on the side of the bed, naked, holding his junk.

Asher shakes his head. "It's true, I was just trying to wake her...your version of waking her was a little nicer," Asher says as he cocks his head and winks at me.

Hunter grits his teeth and glares at Asher. He turns to me to get back into bed when Asher decides to speak again.

"Next time, a heads-up about the early morning sex show would be good...I wouldn't have jerked off in the shower earlier. I would have waited for the show." Asher grins.

My mouth drops open. I swear, he has a death wish right now. Hunter's no longer getting back into bed or holding his junk. He's rushing toward Asher. For fuck's sake, boys are so dumb. Asher's just riling him up, and I have no idea why.

Hunter and Asher are so alike, it's not funny. Maybe that's why I find Asher attractive...because he reminds me of Hunter at times. But right now...this is all Asher.

"Fuck no, if I have to see your dick, I've changed my mind about the show." Hunter has his hand on Asher's throat and he lifts him a little.

But that doesn't deter Asher in any way. "Oh... I'm part of the show too? *Kinky*." He winks at Hunter, who drops him and looks back over to me, wearing a myriad of expressions.

I let out a breath and throw myself back down. "Asher, stop riling Hunter up with your early morning bullshit. I'm getting up once you're out of here."

Asher makes a strangled sound. "No fair, Mila. You're ruining all the fun." He chuckles, and I hear the door slam close.

Opening my eyes, I look over to Hunter, who is staring at the closed door.

"Ignore him, he can be a dick. Just like you."

Hunter turns on me and, with a gleam in his eye, he charges at me, pounding his chest like a caveman. He jumps onto the bed and laughs as he wraps me in his arms and twirls us. The bedding is all caught around me, and I'm pinned.

"My little burrito." He kisses my nose. "I need to leave, but I'll come see you later?"

I nod, and he kisses me quickly before jumping up and reaching for his jeans. "Hey." I wiggle in the sheets.

"Hey, what?" He smirks over at me, and my heart flips.

"I love you."

He stands, his jeans on, a smile beaming over his gorgeous face. The little bit of dark stubble on his chin in the early morning sunlight makes butterflies dance in my belly.

Slowly crawling across the bed, he helps to unwrap me, never taking his eyes from mine. "I love you." He kisses me, and I wrap my arms around his neck.

I don't want to let go. But I don't want him to be

late, and Dad is waiting on Asher to come home so he can drive them both to training.

"Call you later." He jumps up and grabs his tee and other clothing and rushes through the door.

When it closes, I melt into a happy puddle in the bed. I quickly put my clothes back on. I'm glad too, because the quiet in the room doesn't last long.

The door opens and Asher stalks in with a cocky grin, Walker just behind him. "Please take him home, Mila. I love ya, girl, but your boy here is driving me crazy."

I sigh and look between them. Asher's looking all coy and innocent, and I'm growing a little wary of this act.

"What's up with you, Asher? You like Hunter. Why did you mess with him this morning, and don't say it's because it was fun. I thought you were becoming friends and stuff...which, yeah, in the grand scheme of things with the Kings and Rebels rivalry is, well...strange. But you're still human and have feelings. Did you want him to snap your neck?"

Walker turns to Asher. "The fuck, man? What did you say to him to have him wanting to snap your neck?"

Asher shrugs, and I cross my arms. "I won't leave here until you tell me, or I'm telling Dad you wanted to see me naked."

At that, the whole room goes quiet. All I can hear

is the two of them breathing as Walker turns to Asher and nudges him with his shoulder.

Asher throws his hands up and lets out a deep exhale. "Okay…all right. You once asked me if guys and girls can be friends without all the sex shit getting in the way. I told you…"

He takes a step toward me. "My truth. When it comes to you—I want you, I know I shouldn't, but I do. I'll get over it, don't worry, and I'll apologize to Hunter."

Walker just shakes his head and gives Asher a sympathetic look. *Fuck.* I run my hand down my face and stare at my bare feet. I haven't put my sneakers on yet. I thought…he said…I touched his…fuck.

"You know why we can't," I whisper. Why did that come out as a whisper? I look up at him, and he gives me a small smile and shrugs.

"I know why…but it's also an excuse. They would understand. You feel it too?" His hand is outstretched to me.

Do I feel something for him? Yes, but not like how I feel for Hunter. But is what I feel for Hunter because we have history? There's a foundation already built between us. Asher is new; we're only making a history, building a foundation, now.

When I don't say anything, Asher shakes his head. "I'm sorry I acted like a dick. Just chalk it up to jealousy."

I don't like seeing Asher like this. We both agreed

it was just sexual attraction between us…a lot of attraction, but still. He's been an amazing friend, and I guess we've gotten closer than ever since my accident. So much so that even Dad and Kate have mentioned it, and I worried they wouldn't be happy, but they were. I just didn't see this coming.

Did I miss it, or have his feelings been there the whole time? Why would he think I feel it too? I think back over the past week, and it hits me.

"Want to watch a movie with me?" Asher asks as he helps me with the dishes. I'm attempting to dry the pots, and he's getting water everywhere. His white tee is soaked, and I can see the ripples of his abs through it. I suck my lip into my mouth and chastise myself for looking at him. But I'm a girl…who likes the male body. It's hard not to look.

"Huh?" I look up at him, and he has a grin on his face. Shit, did he catch me looking at him? I fumble with the pot, and it crashes to the ground, clanging around. And I freeze. Shit.

"Are you all right in there?" Kate yells out from another room.

We both reply, "Yes."

"Jinx," we both say together, and it breaks the strange spell between us as we laugh together.

I bend down to pick up the pot, and just as I touch the

cool metal, I feel Asher's warm, calloused hand on mine, but he doesn't pull away.

Freezing, I look over to him. He's so close that I can see gold specks in his deep brown eyes that I've never noticed before. They're so pretty. My eyes roam over his face as my hand grows heated under his, but he makes no move to let go.

We just stare at each other, and it's as if time has stilled and we're both frozen in place. The only hints we aren't frozen are the bob of his Adam's apple as he swallows and the small intake of breath I take at the sight.

I feel…

Butterflies. Fuck.

NINETEEN
ROMAN

pack my bag for the fight tonight, jamming what little possessions I have into it. My hands start to shake, and I collapse onto the floor beside my bed. How many times can I do this? How much more before I break? Before Mila came back, I'd been fine. This was my life, and it was enough.

But now...I know I hadn't been living at all. That wasn't a life—going through the motions to stay alive, and for what? To end up here, packing my bag while the sperm donor is out getting his fix. Fighting for money I won't receive because he's already shot it up his arm.

Why do I keep doing this for him?

When is it enough?

I have very little left to give, and I don't want to waste it on people who don't give a shit about me.

The rain has been pelting against the windows for

the past hour. I like the rain; it's soothing. I love the sound it makes against the thin roof and walls of the trailer. When I was little, I used to hide in my room, away from my parents' fighting. Away from the old man on a bender and screaming and ranting at the TV.

If the rain was loud enough, it could drown it all out. I would lie with my head against the wall, close my eyes, and think of her. The girl with the huge smile, who wanted to hug me even though I was mean to her. The girl who never gave up on me. Until she left.

But even then, did she really give up on me? She won't give up on me now. And that's the only thing that's getting me through each day, knowing she will be there, no matter how hard I push against her.

I turned my phone on earlier. Hunter tried to call when I didn't turn up for practice this morning. Even had a missed call from Jace, which I didn't expect. Hunter's usually the one to call and come around to see if I'm okay. Jace doesn't do it on his own usually; he's always with Hunter.

Jace tried to speak to me a few times this week at school, but I just can't. I need everyone and everything I've ever cared for out of my life, including him. Even if he's being an asshole. He always seems to revert to asshole Jace to keep his emotions bottled up. How do I know? I do the same. But I'm not an asshole about it. I just don't talk.

I know he's lashing out at everyone because he made a mistake, and he knows it…a few mistakes, actually. I might not say much, but I'm observant when it comes to my best friends. Jace…he's hurting, deeply. He just can't see that, right now, he's his own enemy. Once he does, he can stop fighting against himself and everything will get better. I just hope he sees it sooner rather than later. I would hate to see him end up like me.

Alone.

Then, there's Hunter. His parents neglect him. Always have. Yeah, he has flashy new shoes all the time and the car to match. But his mom is always drunk, and his dad…hell, I haven't seen him in a year. Neither go to his games, and I think, in some ways, he sees himself in me. Only, I got the trailer park version of his life.

There's a small sound, and I think for a moment it's coming from the trailer behind mine. Maybe Billy out for his rent money. Stupid time to do it; this rain is relentless.

When the pounding on my trailer door starts and doesn't stop, I scream out, "Fuck off, Billy."

I can't deal with his shit now. I don't want to take it out on him—he's not a bad guy—but I need to see my mom first so I can get the rent money. That's if the Amato family hasn't figured out where I hide most of my cash and already stolen it.

The banging continues. "Fuck's sake," I mutter to

myself as I storm out of my room, somewhat glad the old man isn't here. I can't deal with his fucked-up ass right now. He took the rent money from my room and shot it up his arm. It's why we're late, again.

I throw open the trailer door, and it slams with a thud. It's as though the rain knows I have the door open as it starts to pelt down harder and the wind picks up, causing the droplets to come inside. "Billy, the rent is co—*Mila*?"

I freeze. Mila's standing in the torrential rain. She's wearing a dark hoodie and a pair of dark jeans, her blonde hair laying drenched around her face as she hugs her waist with her arms. Her big blue eyes are looking up at me, sad, scared, and something else...I just don't know what. She jumps when she hears a dog bark and my feet are moving before I can register what I'm doing.

When I reach her, she stills. "You're wet."

The corner of her mouth goes up in a smile, and I know she's thinking of the double meaning there. But all I can think of is how drenched she is, and that she needs to be dry and warm.

She shivers, and I wrap my arm around her shoulder, drawing her into me. She's so small, she fits against my body like a glove. Like she belongs there.

I want to shout to the gods, *"What's this bullshit you've sent me? Every time something good comes, you fuck me over. Haven't I experienced enough hurt? Enough pain? When does it stop?"*

It never ends. Because if it did, I would kiss this beautiful soul and keep her with me always.

But thoughts like that are dangerous, especially after the visit I received early this morning from the assholes. The old man has managed to work out an open account with the Amato family and keeps taking what they offer him.

I don't give a shit about him, and they know it. Their words were, *"Blondie got off easy...maybe not so much next time."*

They've discovered my greatest weakness, and now they're exploiting it.

I'd lunged at them, intending to snap their necks, but the clicking from the gun pressed against the back of my head forced me to stop my assault. If I'm dead, who will protect Mila? Hunter? Jace? They don't even know what shit I'm mixed up in. I need to fight to save Mila. If I don't...the Amato's made it clear they will come back for her.

With that thought in my mind, I scan the area around my trailer. Are they out there? Watching me? Making sure I turn up for the fight tonight? The rain wets my hair, and I realize I've been standing in the rain with her pressed to my chest. I need to get her inside before anyone spots her or she gets sick.

Why is she so wet? Where's her car? No time to ask that now. I usher inside and slam the door closed and lock it and take her straight to my room. The rain pounding on the steel frame doesn't let up; it's loud, but I can still hear her rapid breathing. Fuck, is she hurt?

Spinning her, I look down her body. She seems fine. I push the hair from her face, and she blinks up at me. I run my hand over her head, then down the strands of her wet hair. Water drips off her body and onto the floor as she shakes beneath me.

"Mila," I breathe. My mind and heart are at war. My heart yearns to help her, to get her warm and hug her. To never let her go. But my mind wants to kick her out and tell her to run home and stay as far away from me as possible before she gets killed because of me.

But we're like magnets. No matter where she goes, I know we'll make it back to each other. It's inevitable. We're always going to end up here, together. The harder I try to deny what's between us, the more certain I am—she's it for me.

Mila is my end game, and even if I have to wait twenty more years to keep her safe, she's worth waiting for.

Rushing to the bathroom, I grab my towel, and when I return, she's standing in the same spot, shivering. "Mila, what happened?" Something must have happened for her to be standing on my doorstep in the rain like that. Did she get carjacked? *Fuck.*

"I had to see you, see if you were okay. I had a bad dream, and I needed to see you with my own eyes. To know you were okay."

My heart swells. She had to see me. After a bad dream. God, this girl is going to break down all my walls. I take a deep breath and try to calm myself before I beg her to run away and marry me.

I focus on the task at hand—getting her dry—but her clothes are soaked through. "Where did you park your car?" It must have been far for her to get this wet. Or how long was she standing outside my door?

I pull up the hem of her hoodie, hoping if we get this off, then maybe whatever she's wearing under-neath is dry. She can wear something of mine while I drive her back to her car so she can get home and have a long, hot shower.

"My car had a flat tire. I didn't know how to change it, so I left it at home." She gives me a small smile and shrugs, like it's no big deal.

I grab her shoulders, and she looks up at me. Those eyes…they're like looking into the ocean, so much love and hope in them. I can't be angry with her. "You walked all the way from your house? What were you thinking?"

She blinks and wipes her eyes. Is she crying?

"Mila, don't cry. I'm just worried, okay? It scares me that you walked here alone. In the rain. Can you promise me…"

I let go of her shoulders and run my hands down her arms, trying to catch my thoughts before I scare her. I can feel the cast under the damp fabric on her right arm. Fucking hell. That can't get wet. I let go of her for a moment and pull on my hair before pinning her with my gaze. I want her to know how important this is and that I'm not angry but scared.

"Promise me you will never do that again, ever. You call me or call Hunter. Never walk out here alone; this place isn't safe for you. I don't want you here, but that's only to keep you safe. The people who live here are not good. I don't ever want something to happen to you because you were here.

"So, promise to call me, and I will come change your tire, and you will see I'm alright. Okay?"

She nods and glances around my room. It's not much. Fuck, it's nothing compared to her room, but she just glances back at me and gives me a half smile. "You need to turn your phone on. I was scared for you, so I tried to call you. When you didn't answer, I came here looking for you. To make sure you're okay."

She'd been scared for me...because of a bad dream?

"I took a nap and had this feeling something bad was gonna happen to you, and I needed to see you. I know it sounds silly now. I was just scared that I'd lost you, and I can't, Roman. I'm never letting you go."

The statement frightens me more than I want to admit. After what happened earlier with those two assholes...I could have been killed because my father can't stop and doesn't care about his son. He doesn't care if they kill me. As long as he gets his fix, he would let them. Just like they know that I would do anything to keep Mila safe.

Just eighteen months—that's all I need and I will be done. I will move into the club...or choose a different path.

One without pain and hurt.

One that includes Mila.

TWENTY
MILA

'd dropped Asher off at his place and said hi to Dad. Asher didn't speak in the car at all, and neither did I. I didn't know what to say. He thanked me for the lift, then I left for home.

I needed time to think about what he'd said. It was all too much. So much shit had gone down since I moved back home. Jace, Roman, Hunter, now Asher and Grady. I'm starting to think I'm cursed. Everything I touch turns to shit. Well, not Hunter—he's my gold. I finally drifted off to sleep, but it was fitful, my dream dark.

Actually, it was more a bad feeling about Roman. It seemed so real, the feelings washing over me all dark and twisted, like I knew something bad is going to happen to him. Like, really bad. And I need to stop it. Were those guys back? Did they want to hurt him?

We haven't spoken about them, but I worry about it every day.

Even though it sounds silly when I explain everything to him, I'm glad I came, if only to see with my own two eyes that he's safe. Except, now that I'm here, I don't want to leave. I can't imagine leaving him behind. His room is neat and tidy, for what there is in here—a few football trophies, a poster of Metallica on his wall, his neatly made bed, and an old, broken dresser. It isn't much, but Roman's whole life is in this room.

The rest of the place doesn't look like this. I can tell his father never cleans. He must fall asleep with his cigarettes still lit, as there are ash and burn marks in the carpet around his chair. I don't think he even cooks. Roman probably does the bulk of that as well. It makes me so angry that Roman has to take care of himself and his father, where for most kids it's the other way around.

Roman clears his throat. "Let's get you dry," he mumbles under his breath.

I'd been worried that he would send me home the moment he saw me. Maybe if it hadn't been raining, he would have. I smile to myself. Roman cares about me. He wants me to promise to never come here alone. I won't. I'd never been so scared in my life. If it weren't for the rain, I'm not sure if I would have made it here. Most people weren't dumb enough to run around in it.

"Yeah, that would be great. I'm freezing." I shiver because of how cold I actually am.

The wind had a slight chill to it when I had left home, and I'd been gone about twenty minutes before I realized the mistake I made with the weather. But I'd refused to turn back, not until I could see Roman with my own eyes.

"Should've packed an umbrella." I try to lighten the mood.

The tension between us is so heavy, it's weighing down my chest. I want to hug him, to kiss him. But I hold myself still; he doesn't want those things. Roman doesn't even smile at my words. He's really upset about me coming here alone.

He grabs the hem of my hoodie again, and this time, I raise my arms as he pulls it up and over my head. It gets caught on my cast, and we both slowly peel the fabric off.

I didn't realize how bad my cast is until I see it. Crap. I really shouldn't have kept walking in the rain. It seems fine inside, just the outside is a little softer than it should be. I'm going to the hospital next week for a checkup, and they can decide if I need a new one. If anything, I want to take it off and scratch my arm.

He holds the towel out for me and looks down at my jeans. They're so wet, they are going to be hard to take off without help. Taking a step back, he turns his back on me and pulls something out of his bag. He turns back to me with a dry hoodie, one I've seen him wear many times.

"You can wear this to keep warm, and I'll drive you home. Fix your car's tire."

I nod in thanks, but I don't want to leave just yet. Once I'm home, he will help me fix the tire, but then he'll leave. I want to keep this, whatever *this* is, for longer. Just to sit here and talk or listen to him. I know he's not much of a talker. But anything I can get, just silence with him beside me, is all I need right now.

I take my time trying to dry my hair as best I can. My t-shirt is damp, but it will dry. My hoodie will need to be put in a dryer, and I doubt I'll find one at Roman's place.

Jamming my right arm into the hoodie is a struggle. The cast is tight in the sleeve, even though it's so big. I think it's just catching onto the fabric. Once I have it on, it swamps my body, and it smells just like Roman.

I try to sniff it discreetly, but when I look over, I see him watching me with a puzzled expression. I smile and shrug. So what, sue me. I love the smell of him.

The fact that he'd given me a hug and touched me more times in the last ten minutes than he has since I've been back says something. He wants to, and he's holding back to protect me from all this bad shit. It breaks my heart that he thinks he has to protect me. Shouldn't I be able to make that choice for myself?

Thinking back to that kiss at Jace's house—the one where he pressed me against the door—I lick my lips, wanting to chase after that memory right now.

Roman takes a step toward me, his eyes roaming my face, before he pushes some of my hair behind my ear. He gives me a crooked smile and my belly flip-flops with butterflies. "Are you warm?"

I smile. I wish I could keep his hoodie, but I know he doesn't have a lot. And as much as I want to snuggle up with it at night, I have to give it back to him.

My pulse picks up as he steps closer again. His chin rests on my head as he tugs me into a bear hug. I hadn't been expecting it so my arms are pinned to my sides. I want to touch him, but maybe he did it this way so I wouldn't.

He pulls back a little, and I do the same, looking up at him. His eyes watch me as he tilts his head slightly, his hair falling from behind his ear as he moves in close. Our foreheads touch, and his hair is like a curtain to the outside world. In here, nothing can hurt us.

His eyes close, and I follow suit as I feel the soft touch of his lips against mine. I go with him, not wanting to stop. It's soft and slow, nothing like the kiss we shared against that door. No, this is like the kiss we shared on the road.

My last kiss.

Is this what this is? Is he giving me my last kiss again? It isn't a kiss goodbye from me. This is only the beginning. I reach my left hand up and between us. My fingers snake around his neck, and I feel him tense under my touch.

If this is my last kiss, I'm going to make it the best one.

Pulling him closer to me, he opens his mouth. My tongue sweeps over his, and we kiss like we are at war. One waving a white flag and the other still fighting. I won't let us end like this. I don't care what he thinks. I'm safer when I'm with him.

I bite his lip, and he lets out a hiss. I open my eyes to see the fire burning behind his as he grips my waist and pulls me against him. The wet jeans feel heavy against my skin. But so does he. It's impossible to miss the hardness against my belly.

We stand there, our breaths mingling as we stare each other down. Nothing but the sound of the rain and my heart beating.

"Mila, I—"

The door to the trailer slams open and shut, and I jump in Roman's arms. He turns me, pushing me behind his body as he stands tall, ready for anything.

I can feel him trembling under my hand. I'm not sure if it's me or the person out there that's making him shake, but I don't want to let go of Roman.

"Where's the rent, boy?" Damon calls out in the

other room as another door slams shut. I hear what sounds like a bottle cap, and I think Roman's father is out there, drinking a beer.

"Come, grab your stuff. I'll take you home."

Gone is the Roman from a few moments again. He's rebuilt his walls and is back to the standoffish Roman he's been all week. He takes my hand, which surprises me, as we leave his room. The smell of his father hits me, and I want to gag. Has the guy never showered?

His father turns to me and smiles. I want to throw up at the sight. It's not a friendly smile.

"Oh, hello there again, sweet thang."

We don't say anything as Roman opens the door to the pouring rain.

"Aww, don't leave. I bet I'm a lot more fun than he was."

Yep, throwing up now.

TWENTY-ONE
MILA

Spirit week. The school is covered in red and black posters and streamers. Everyone is pumped for the homecoming game on Friday against the West Maitland Wildcats. It's going to be a great game; they're an amazing team, so the Rebels have their work cut out for them. But I know we can win this.

Well, we could if Jace wasn't still fighting with the guys...hell, half the team. His own brother still isn't talking to him, and I have no idea how this is going to go down. The team is more fractured than ever.

Jace has pissed off the guys who are loyal to Grady, while others now look at Grady like he's going to watch them changing in the locker room or come on to them. *Assholes*. So, there's a divide in the team, and it all comes back to Jace and Britney. They equally damaged the team's morale.

The cheerleaders are extra bouncy today. Guess they're trying to get dates for the homecoming dance on Saturday. I technically don't have a date. I know Hunter will be mine, but he hasn't asked, so until he does, I'm not going with him. I'm going solo.

"Mila, do you want to go dress shopping after school today? I wasn't gonna go to the dance, but now…" Cadence glances around the table we're seated at in the cafeteria and smiles.

"I'm going," Sadie says. "We should do a girls' night, get ready together, and all go together. It will be fun."

I nod in agreement, loving that idea. It will be nice to have some girl time. I've never had many female friends before…like, ever. I love what I have with these girls. The friendship is growing stronger each day, and we can talk about so much shit, like boys and how dumb they can be.

Hunter wraps his arm around my shoulder and pulls me against him. I inhale his scent and sigh a little at how yummy he always smells. "Aww…I thought we were going together, babe?"

I lean into him and pat his leg. He chuckles and shakes his head. He knows what that means; he won't win this round.

"Okay, but I get to dance with you."

I kiss him, and Emerson groans at the public display. He's told us to stop kissing in front of him, since it makes him sad that he has no one to kiss. I told him to kiss my ass, and he actually tried. He got down on his knees, and Hunter bonked him on the head for even thinking he could kiss my ass.

"Of course, you get to dance with me, and shut up, Emerson."

"I want a kiss," he mumbles, and I chuckle. Hunter jerks against me and there is an "*oomph*" from Emerson.

I look over and see Emerson rubbing the back of his head. I pat Hunter's chest and shake my head.

Cadence told me Emerson laid down some pickup lines last Friday at the game. I laughed so hard when she told me she turned him down. I'd warned her and Sadie that the boys on the team are awesome, but they have big egos, and most are manwhores. If they're looking for a one-night stand, then go crazy. But there are only a few that are boyfriend material, and those have girlfriends already.

She took my advice and decided to say no to Emerson. She said he's cute, but she doesn't want to give up her V-card to just some guy on the football team. She's not that kind of girl. And if Emerson ever did her wrong, I would have his nuts in a vise. I think he knows it because he didn't push her. He actually said, and I quote, *"I respect that and hope to see you Monday at lunch."*

What the hell? I asked her if he was hit on the head during the game and wasn't thinking straight.

Sadie told me that's exactly what he said, and they were both surprised. Maybe he isn't a lost cause after all. Hunter said that Emerson had fucked most of the cheerleaders. I'm sure Hunter has too. But that's the past.

Jace comes out of nowhere and takes a seat at the table. I don't like the way he's looking today. He looks rough, and I worry about him. He doesn't speak to anyone; he just puts his head down to eat. This is different from the cocky and so-sure-of-himself Jace from weeks ago. Someone needs to talk to him. I pat Hunter's leg and gesture for him to go over there, but he shakes his head. Guys can be so stubborn.

Jace looks up under his lashes at me and catches my eye. I'm the only one watching him right now, and I want to scream out, "Fix the mess you made." All he has to do is fix things with Grady then Hunter. Whatever it is, they will forgive him if he apologizes. I know that. As much as Jace hurt me, he doesn't deserve this.

Finally, he blinks and turns away, and I look back to Cadence, who's talking about the color of the dress she wants. I tell her and Sadie about a red dress I saw in the window of the boutique at the mall. Sadie thinks it's my color, and I have to agree. I think Rebels red suits me.

"Jace, there's no room, move over."

I turn with the rest of the table to see Britney and

Summer standing behind Jace, holding their trays with sour expressions on their faces.

Jace looks behind at them, shakes his head, and drops it again. "Just leave, there's no room," he mutters just loud enough for me to hear.

"But you're the quarterback, Jace. You can make them move," she whines.

I look at Grady. His jaw is ticking, and I can see he's upset.

Jace, whenever you don't have balls...it's always with Britney around. No one likes her. Can't you see she's bad for you?

When he doesn't answer, I do. "You're not wanted here. Just go, Britney."

Her nose scrunches up, and she sneers toward me, Sadie, and Cadence. "You let two losers sit at your table. They're no one. How pathetic."

I internally say to myself, *Just be nice, don't say a thing, and ignore her like everyone else.*

"Get up, losers, make room for us. You're in our spots. Make them move. Emerson, make them move."

Emerson starts to stand, and I'm just done. I stand up too and turn to Britney. "Britney, no one wants you here. You hang around unwanted...like *herpes*."

The whole table laughs together at that, and I smirk at her. I hate being mean; I never want to be a bully, but I'm done with her.

Britney just stands there, her mouth gaping open

like she didn't think I had any fight in me. I've ignored her all week. Let her play her childish shit with Jace. But if she wants to start messing with my friends for no reason other than to be mean, that's a hell no from me. Sadie and Cadence don't deserve it. Britney is the loser. No one wants to sit with someone with such a bad attitude.

I take a seat and turn back to the girls, who are holding their hands over their mouths. But I can see the smile in their eyes.

"So, anyway, I was thinking we should paint my cast to match. Get rid of some of the dick drawings on there." They merely blink at me. I guess I just went from zero to one hundred and back again.

"Do you need help?" Hunter asks me, and he holds my fingers and gently turns my hand over so he can see the underside. He rubs his thumb over one of the little dicks he drew on there yesterday.

"Not from you. You'll just draw more dicks on there."

He chuckles, and Emerson does too. They high-five. Boys are so childish.

"You should ask Roman. He's good at tattoos. He's gotta be good with a paintbrush too."

I kiss Hunter and smile.

. . .

As soon as Roman drove me home Saturday, I called and told Hunter what had happened. He gave me the same lecture about walking to the trailer park in the rain.

Hunter came over, and we talked about everything. How Roman and I kissed, and how it made me feel. It was weird at first, telling my boyfriend I kissed his best friend. But he just smiled and even said, "Good for Roman," which made it easier.

I know my wanting to not choose between them is hard for Hunter. It would be hard on anyone. But I'm glad that Hunter is so on board with it all. Even now, telling me to go ask Roman. To spend more time with him. I love that about Hunter. He cares for everyone. And I care for him.

Still, I didn't tell him about Asher. That's…a clusterfuck.

Are my butterflies off-kilter? When I saw Asher on Sunday at dinner, they had been there. They were small in my belly, but they were there. Maybe they'd been there all along, and I'd pushed them down so far because I didn't feel them. Not until Saturday morning, and now that's all I can see and feel. *Butterflies.* I'm so confused and conflicted.

Asher watched me when he didn't think I was watching him, but I was. Our usual, impassioned conversations over the dinner table had been reduced to, "Can you pass the beans?" And everyone picked up on it. I told them I was tired, and Asher did the same. Which only made them even more suspicious.

I won't have to see Asher tonight if I'm with the girls, since I can have dinner out with them. But I can't avoid this topic forever. I have to tell Hunter. If only I knew what to tell him. Just that Asher wants to be more than friends? That I do? I don't know if I do. I'm lost on this one.

Maybe some girl talk tonight will help me clear it up. I can't go to Asher about my guy problems anymore. Maybe Grady can help me? My stomach aches; there's too much going on, and I don't know what to do. Every smile Hunter has given me today reminds me that not only am I lying to him about the accident, but I'm lying about Asher and me as well.

I need to be the one to tell Hunter. Before Asher apologizes to him and tells Hunter the truth about why he was a dick.

Why is this so fucking messed up?

bought the dress, and it's perfect. More than perfect, and Hunter is going to love it with the big slit up the side. I hope Roman comes to the dance. I tried to talk to him today after school about painting my cast, but he just nodded and walked away like I was finished talking. Does that mean he's going to help me?

Since the heels I got to wear with the dress are black and silver, the girls and I decided that we should paint the cast to match them. Sadie suggested that I should use a silver marker to draw the moon and stars on it. The theme for the dance is star-crossed lovers and it would be so perfect.

Which means I need Roman to be there more than ever.

There's a knock at the front door, and I run down the stairs. Hunter's coming over. Dad said he can't stay long and that he will be home soon. And not to go into my bedroom alone with him. Hello, Dad. Sex doesn't just happen in bedrooms. We can do it almost anywhere. But I didn't tell him that. I'm glad he's cool with Hunter being here with me. Alone.

I open the door to find a single red rose on my front step. Reaching down, I pick it up and smell it. It's beautiful, but who gave it to me? I look around and don't see Hunter's car.

"Hunter?" I call out. But there's no one.

Oh my god. Roman? Could this have been from him? We used to pick daisies, and he would place one behind my ear. Is this his way of asking me to the dance? I told him I'm getting a dress in Rebels red and wanted the cast black. My heart speeds up a little as I turn with a huge grin on my face.

Hunter's car pulls up just as I start to walk inside, so I rest my shoulder against the doorframe and watch as he strides over to me. He wraps his arms around me, and I squeal as he swings me around.

"A rose. For me, how sweet." He chuckles then kisses me before setting me back on the porch.

"No, I think it's from Roman. I think he put it there and just left."

Hunter nods, but I can see he's a bit unsure as he looks to Jace's house.

Oh shit. How did I not think that it could have been Jace? After the way he was at lunch today, he might be trying to make up for all his wrongs, and a rose is a sweet gesture. But words and, more importantly, actions are the only things he can give me right now.

"Come on." I tug on Hunter's tee. "Let's go to my room before my dad gets home."

Screw the rule. I want Hunter between my thighs right now and to forget about all the bullshit in the world.

His deep chuckle has me smiling like crazy. He bends down and lifts me over his shoulder and smacks my ass.

Sorry, Dad...*not sorry.*

The marching band is playing for a packed stadium. Sadie is jumping up and down beside me, wearing one of the matching tops the three of us bought for the game—all Rebels red. I love calling it that.

She's pointing at Hunter, and I smile at her as she winks at me. Then she points at one of the guys in the band, but I can't figure out who as I try to scream over at her. My voice is drowned out by all the noise. Everyone's excited to watch the game tonight.

Friday night lights.

Even better—it's homecoming.

Everyone and their mom is here. It's a huge turnout, and I didn't want to miss it, especially since Hunter and Roman have no family but me here. I'll be their support system. Their family.

Eventually, the chaos dies down a bit, and the

cheerleaders are doing their thing. I watch Hunter; he's laughing with Grady and Emerson. Grady seems more himself tonight which makes me happy. I can't see Roman at first, then I spot him. He's sitting alone, and it breaks my heart to see him so down. I wanted to braid his hair for the game, but he wouldn't let me.

He did paint my cast black today. I'd been surprised at lunch when he came up and nodded for me to follow him. He took me out to the grassy area where we'd been sitting together before the accident. I know he hasn't been sitting here without me; I've been checking.

Pulling out a small paint container and a paint-brush, he got to work. I tried to talk to him. After Saturday and that kiss, I wanted to push for a little more. But he only gave me a few grunts and didn't hug me. I'd been sad about the no hug thing. I wanted a Roman hug so badly.

The cheerleaders finish their routine on the field, and the guys are all getting ready. Hunter's ass is looking mighty fine from where I'm sitting. He looks over and he sees me, and I blow him a kiss. I know he's trying to concentrate, so I haven't been trying to get his attention. This is an important game for him and for the entire school.

Music starts playing, and I see Hunter dancing along while listening to the coach. He's an amazing dancer. Coach moves back a little, and Zack and Leo start dancing beside Hunter. I hold in my laugh as the coach eyes them, and they don't seem to notice, or they do and don't care. The three of them are doing some dance all in sync, like they've been practicing it for weeks. It's quite funny. Coach isn't impressed, but I see him crack a smile and shake his head when they finish.

"Are you a good dancer?" Cadence asks me.

I chuckle. "Hunter's dancing skills are way above mine. I have some rhythm, but I can't do that." I stare down at him with dreamy eyes. I know I look like a lovestruck fool. But that's because I am.

"Is Leo single?" Sadie randomly asks.

"I'm not sure. What about the marching band guy?" I ask, and her cheeks turn red. "No way. Sadie. Who is it? You were pointing, and he was …marching." I giggle. I couldn't follow her gesture because they were moving, so I'm not sure which one caught her eye.

Cadence doesn't waste a second in jumping into the conversation. "Tyler Hall—he's a senior."

I don't know him, but now I want to, if he's making Sadie's cheeks turn Rebels red. I have to bite back a smile. Maybe I should stop calling the color red *Rebels red*.

"You have a photo? His Instagram?" Everyone has Instagram.

Cadence is on it before I can even finish, and Sadie groans, her hands on her face.

"No, don't get embarrassed. You pointed…now

you need to tell me. How long have you had a crush on him?"

"Since I was a freshman." My eyes meet hers and she smiles now. "He's so cute and smart. I fell over in the hallway, and he helped me up. Asked if I was okay and smiled at me."

Aww…that's so sweet.

Cadence shows me his photo, and he is cute. He has that Harry Styles look about him—not the fashion, but his face and hair.

"Why don't you ask him to the homecoming dance?" Sadie looks at me like she's going to be sick. Shit. I hold my hand out to hers. "It's okay, don't freak out. Maybe we can ask Hunter."

They both look at me with a puzzled expression.

"He knows, like…everyone." I wave my hand around to emphasize it. "I can't even walk to class without him saying hello to everyone we pass. I'm sure he knows Tyler."

They give me looks like they don't believe me, but I leave it. I'll get Sadie a dance with Tyler. I'm going to be her wingwoman at the dance tomorrow.

The game gets off to a great start. Our offense starts, and Jace snaps the ball and passes it to Roman for a running play. I cheer, screaming out his name. He doesn't get far, but that's okay.

They set the play up again, and it's the same. Roman runs, pressing past the Wildcats defense. "Go, Roman, go," I scream at the top of my lungs.

Holy shit, Roman's sprinting down the field, and the Wildcats can't catch him. I'm holding my breath. *Run, you got this.*

Touchdown for the Rebels.

I jump and scream, hugging Cadence and Sadie. I'm so excited. With a start to the game like that, we're gonna win…

The Rebels have this.

The Rebels didn't have it. They lost, thirty-nine to seventeen. The Wildcats must have noticed the tension between Jace and Grady, and they played on that. As the game went on, Grady changed on the field. Whatever they said to him noticeably affected his game. It was hard to watch. I wanted to go out there and kick their asses.

"So, how many stars do you want on your cast?" Cadence asks as she finishes up drawing the moon on there. The silver looks amazing; she's really good at this. Apparently, she likes to draw anime. She'll have to teach me once my arm is healed. It would be fun to get back into drawing.

"Make it two. I only have one star-crossed lover."

Sadie giggles. "I can't believe you're trying to

hook up with Roman while you're dating Hunter. Like, holy shit, you're crazy. In all the best ways. I love this. Do you think he'll show?"

I hope so because I want to see him. I want to dance with him and Hunter.

"I'm not holding my breath. It's pretty much impossible to predict what Roman will do. Also, I'm not trying to hook up with him. He's mine, like, as in the *forever* type of mine."

He just refuses to see it and keeps trying to sacrifice himself for me. I don't need saving—he does.

There's a knock at the front door. I look down to where Cadence is finishing the last star, and I jump up off the bed. With a twirl, I show the girls the cast as I walk out the door. "Looks amazing, thank you."

I carefully walk down the stairs; my dress is long, and I don't want to trip and fall. I smile, my heart overflowing with giddy happiness. I'm so excited to watch Hunter's face when he sees me in this dress, but that better not be him now. He promised I'd meet him there. Sadie's driving us…then he can drive me home after.

Opening the door, I find two red roses on the step. I freeze. My hand still on the door handle, I just stare at them. The last one wasn't from Hunter, and I'd thought it might have been from Roman, but Hunter didn't seem so convinced that Roman was sneaking over and dropping off roses on my doorstep.

Jace? I looked over at his house. The lights are on

and his parents are home. I see Jace's car but not Grady's.

Fuck, I think Hunter might be right. But why the hell is Jace giving me roses? I take them inside and upstairs, and the girls squeal at them.

"Are they from Hunter?" Sadie asks.

I shake my head and place them on my night-stand. Sitting on the edge of my bed, I reach for my heels and start putting them on.

"Roman?" Cadence sits beside me and does up the straps of her small heel.

"No, Hunter thinks it's Jace."

I see the puzzled expression on Sadie's face.

"This isn't the first rose. I got one last Saturday. Now I have two more." I'm trying to find the meaning behind them. Why is he giving me two tonight? Is that Jace's way of saying sorry and he wants me to be his...what? Friend? Girlfriend? Not happening.

"But let's not think about that. I spoke to Hunter, and he knows Tyler and said he will 'set it up.'"

Cadence squeals so loudly my ear rings. I rub it and she mutters, "Sorry," but then she jumps up, wobbling on her heels, and jumps a few times. "This is it, Sadie. You have to dance with him. Maybe go on a date with him?"

Sadie has her arms wrapped tightly around her waist and is shaking her head and mouthing, "No."

We're both nodding yes, but it doesn't seem to

help. Maybe I overstepped and she's not ready for this. Or maybe she's just an introvert and needs a little push?

"Okay, what if we do nothing and nothing happens, and he graduates, and you never get to find out if he was your forever, and now you're forty, alone and sad because you never took the chance at the homecoming dance to be with the sweet and cute Tyler Hall?"

Cadence snorts. "You paint a pretty picture there, Mila."

I shrug. "I try." Then I poke my tongue out at her.

Sadie paces a few times and, finally, she stands straight with a smile on her face. "I can do this. If he wants to dance with me, I will."

I smile and let out a deep breath. "Oh good, because when I said Hunter will set it up..." They both look at me, and I smile. "Tyler's going to come up to you and ask you to dance. He's expecting you to say yes, so please don't say no. Hunter said he's kinda shy, so please tell me now if you're going to say no so I can give the guy a heads-up."

Sadie holds her hand over her mouth and shakes her head, then nods, then shakes, and I'm confused if that's a yes or a no.

"Yes, I will say yes." And she jumps around with Cadence.

Standing up, I walk around the room in my heels.

I prefer my sneakers; these things will be killing me by the end of the night.

"Let's go get our dance on," I call out behind the girls as we all file out and down the stairs. At the last moment, I change my mind and ditch the heels. Cadence laughs as she watches me slide my foot in my sneaker and sigh.

"I told you, the higher the heel, the greater the pain." She *tsks* at me.

I shake my head and smile up at her as I slip my other foot in. "My mother taught me, pain is beauty. I'm used to wearing heels for all her stupid functions. I don't know why I even bought them, to be honest. Old habit, I guess. I forgot I can be my own person here. If my mom saw me wearing sneakers, she would drop dead." And that's the truth.

I double-check my small bag—I have my phone, purse, keys, lip gloss, and eyeliner, just in case. You never know when you need to touch up, and I did my favorite smoky eyes. God, if Mom could see me now.

Closing the door behind me, I bounce over to Sadie's red coupe, something I never could have done in those death traps women call heels. Cadence is in the back so I can sit up front. My dress is too tight to squish back there and not rip the slit higher. As I get to the car door, my phone starts to ring. I open my bag and see the caller ID.

Roman.

I quickly answer and put it to my ear. "Roman?" There's no sound at first, then I hear his dad, yelling, and something smashing. *Shit.*

"Roman?" My throat grows thick as my hand flies to my chest to stop my heart from beating out of my chest.

"Please, are you okay?" I choke out.

Why doesn't he say something? He never calls me. Why is he calling me now? Does he need me? I hear him breathing, his voice deep and raspy, like he's been screaming for hours.

"I love you," is all he says. Then it disconnects.

"Roman," I scream at the phone as I try to call him back, but it goes straight to voicemail. *Fuck. Shit.* This is bad.

Two sets of eyes are on me, and my hands shake as I search my bag for my car keys.

"We can drive you," Sadie calls out, and I shake my head.

The last thing Roman would want is two other people from school seeing where he lives. Plus, with the three of us turning up dressed like this, the scary guys there would have the time of their life. Like they won a prize at the damn fair.

"No, go to the dance. I will go see if he's okay, and I'll meet you there."

Please be okay, please be safe, Roman. I'm coming for you.

...I love you too.

TWENTY-THREE
ROMAN

I had to win.

The homecoming game had been full of so much positive energy. I'd wanted to enjoy it, but I couldn't. I had to win this game. I couldn't lose. Losing wasn't an option.

Pinkie and Zero were there in the crowd to cheer me on. They came to watch me. Just as Mila had; she smiled and waved at me, and I turned my back on her. Because they weren't the only people there to see me play.

The Amato family was there too. Johnny and Carlo. They are the two thugs who seem to come visit when they want something from me. They're a noose around my neck, and I'm barely breathing. But no one catches on. No one can see this secret I hold close to my chest. Except Mila. I can't get anything past her. That's why I need to turn my back on her; show no emotion, and she won't get hurt.

But I failed. I did everything right, but our defense crumbled. I scored. I did my best, but Grady couldn't hold them back. He had an off game.

We lost…and now I'm paying for it.

I look up into Carlo's eyes; they're cold and calculating as he cocks his head. He presses the gun against my head a little harder. The cold metal digs in more, and all I can think of is her. The way her face lights up when she sees me, like I'm her favorite person in the world.

Johnny is yelling, and I see Mila running from me, laughing. Wearing that pretty white dress as we pick daisies together. A fist to the jaw has my head spinning to the side, and I see her giggling as she blows on a dandelion, and we watch as the seeds spiral away into the wind.

"*Make a wish*," she says in that sweet voice.

And I smile. I wish to be happy…I wish for this to be over.

"What the fuck you grinning at, kid?" Carlo spits at me, and I'm back to reality. Where there is no happy, and no end.

I'm pushed to the floor. I groan and spit up blood. The sound of boots stomping as they leave the trailer barely registers. My father—the worthless piece of shit—is staring at me as I roll around, groaning. I hurt everywhere.

I can see him moving his lips, but I can't hear him. A blow to the side of my head has my ears still ringing as I blink up at him, a broken son lying on the floor. Wishing he had one caring bone in his body to protect me. To fight for me. But why now, after sixteen, almost seventeen, years would he care for me?

Such a sad way to die. Here, in this shitty trailer, on a dirty carpet with my father yelling at me about drugs, because that's all he cares about. What else is he going to yell or talk to me about?

I close my eyes and sleep.

wake to sunlight and my father sleeping in his chair. I watch his chest rise and fall, wishing it wouldn't. I've been here all night, lying here, bleeding and injured, and he didn't help.

I struggle to get up. They did a lot of damage, mostly internal. I guess they don't want to fully kill me. Just teach me a lesson. So I can fight for them again, play football, be their toy monkey.

I drag myself to my room and lie on my bed. The pain in my left hand is unbearable. Looking down, I see two of my fingers are dislocated, and I think they fractured my little finger. I bite down on my pillow as I put them back in place.

With a muffled roar, I pass out from the pain.

· · ·

hear my father. It's night again. I'm still not dead. I haven't eaten or had anything to drink in twenty-four hours. Last night, I got back after the game and was met by Carlo and Johnny.

My body shakes from the lack of everything. I feel hot and clammy. I'm thirsty, so thirsty. I get up, my body screaming at me as I make my way to the kitchen to get some water and food, if I can stomach it.

"Oh good, you're up. We're out of beer. I need cash."

I waver on my feet and blink over at him, seeing two of him. *Fuck*. I hold on to a chair as my head spins, and I feel a hot flush run through my body. I think I'm about to faint.

"Did you hear me, boy?"

When I don't answer, he gets up and shoves me. I stumble back and crash onto the floor. I try to concentrate on breathing as my vision grows dark, and I don't want to pass out in front of him. He'll probably beat me while I'm unconscious.

"You gonna die?" he asks casually, like he's asking about the weather.

I look up at him. The eyes reflecting back make me shiver.

"If so, tell me where you stash your cash so I can get beer."

I scream. Everything I have, I scream at him...at the world. "Fuck you!" I'm done.

I get up and shove him. He takes a swing, and I block it. I hit him as he stumbles, but he doesn't seem to register the hit, the drugs in his system making him feel nice and good. While every bone in my body screams at me in pain.

Only, I don't have the energy to fight him, and he gets in a few cheap shots. I stumble my way back to my room. He's screaming out at me, calling me a pussy. If anyone's the pussy, it's him. Only a weak man would beat down his injured son.

I listen to him rant and rave for ten minutes before I pick up my phone and dial Mila.

I need her to be safe, and if I'm not here anymore, she'll be safe...right? When I'm no longer an Amato puppet, there will be no reason to hurt her. I need her to know how much I love her. That she's my world; I only exist for her.

But as soon as I hear her voice, I know *I can't*. I can't leave her here alone with men like my father and the Amato family out there. She needs someone to protect her. I have to fight for her.

"Roman?" she calls out, and I whisper the words I have wanted to tell her every day since she gave me that very first hug.

"I love you." I disconnect the call and turn off my phone.

A tear rolls down my face, and I wipe it away. My

hair covers my eyes, so I brush it back behind my ear and sag into the mattress. Closing my eyes, I see her splashing water at me and messing up my hair, just so she can push it behind my ear.

Her giggles, the way she scrunches her nose at pineapple on pizza. The way she bites her lip when she's thinking, the way that...

I love Mila Hart.

TWENTY-FOUR

MILA

By the time I make it to the trailer park, it's dark and scarier than it is during the day. I shrink behind the steering wheel as I make my way down to Roman's trailer.

I see the little white car he's been driving and park beside it. After turning off the ignition, I take a deep breath. I'm worried about what I'll find inside that trailer, and I need to be brave right now. I can't be scared. In order to help Roman, I need to put on my big girl panties and get in there.

As I exit my car, the night air wraps around me in a chilling hug. I hope it's not a premonition of the night. Roman is strong. He has to be okay.

But how long can one person be strong without breaking?

I take a few steps forward and almost fall face-first because the length of the dress makes it hard to move fast. I wish I'd changed before coming here. The dress exposes me more than I would like out here. I'm just glad I have sneakers on. At least I can get to the car faster than in heels if I need to.

I lock my car and hold my keys in my hand, quickly adjusting them so that two keys are sticking out of my fisted hand. It's a tip I'd seen on YouTube for women walking alone at night. Two keys. I would feel a little better if I didn't have to use my left hand, but it's better than nothing.

The porch of the trailer is dark, but the window beside it glows with the faint light of a TV. His father must be here. Damon's done something to him—I'm sure of it.

I knock and stand back, waiting for the vile man to appear.

He doesn't take long, slamming the door open and squinting to see me. "You got beer?" he asks, and I think, at first, he hasn't recognized me.

I take a deep breath and stand tall. "No, I'm here to take Roman."

And I am. There's no way I'm letting him live here another day. If he doesn't come with me, I'm calling Child Protective Services myself. I know he doesn't want that, but I just can't see him like this anymore. He would be better off anywhere but here.

"Ah, pussy boy is licking his wounds in his room. Come in, sweet thang."

I cringe at the way he says *sweet thang*. He lingers at the door and it has me tightening the fisted keys. They hurt my hand, but it's nothing like the hurt he could inflict on me. When he doesn't move, I slide past him.

His fingertip strokes along the back of my arm, and I shrink away from him. I don't stop walking until I'm standing outside Roman's door. I turn back to see his father has closed the door, and he's eyeing me, rubbing his chin.

I swallow down the thick lump in my throat and knock. "Roman? Are you in there? Are you okay?"

There's a pained groaning sound coming from the room. I don't hesitate—I open the door. It's dark, but I can see his figure lying on the bed in a fetal position.

My heart sinks. What has he ever done to this world? Why must he go through so much pain? *I'm done*. I'm going to get Roman away from here and call the police.

"Pussy boy's not up for much, but I am." His dad leers from the doorway, and all the hairs on my body stand at attention.

Roman tries to say something, but all I can hear is *whooshing* in my ears. All I can see is red. I slam the door in his father's face.

"Roman." I rush to his side. "Oh god, what has he done to you?" My hands hover above his injured body. He's shaking, and I can't stop the tears from falling. "It's okay. I'm here now. I'm going to protect you from him."

Shifting, I find his backpack on the floor. I quickly flip on the light, but I hesitate before turning back around. If I see Roman right now, I'm worried I will run out there and kill that man myself. So, instead, I open the backpack and get busy putting his belongings in there.

Whatever we don't get now, I'll buy for him. I never want him to come back here again. I pick up a leather vest. I've never seen that before. Flipping it around, I see that it says *The Sons of Death MC* and *Prospect*.

My heart stops for a moment. Is Roman part of all that? I've seen those guys running around town on their bikes, but never, for a moment, did I think Roman would join them. Why would he want to join them...unless it's for protection or to stop bad shit from happening? Are the guys who hit me part of this motorcycle club?

I don't have time to ask him, so I shove it in the bag. It must be important to him. Letting out a deep, shaking breath, I turn to face Roman.

His dirty-blond hair is plastered to his face, and he's red in the face and shaking uncontrollably. Even only in his boxers, he looks so small, so...unwell. I see the bruises on his body. I rush over and place my hand on his forehead.

"You're burning up. You have a fever, Roman."

Fucking hell, if I didn't come here, who would have helped him? His father sure wouldn't. Would The Sons of Death come and help him?

He reaches out to me, his hands shaking, and I can see the bruised knuckles where he fought back. Gently taking one of his hands in mine, I turn it palm side up, place my cheek on his palm, and kiss it.

"I'll take care of you, Roman. I'm going to take you home. This isn't your home anymore; you will come live with me." Dad will agree. He has to. Roman can't stay here one more day.

He shakes his head. "Mila, no. I can't. They'll find where you live."

Who's *they*? The motorcycle gang? They can come and find me all they want; I don't give a shit. I will fight them.

"Let me help you put some clothes on." I find a pair of sweats in a pile beside him. There's a t-shirt there as well.

He shakes his head again, but I ignore his protests.

"I'm doing this, whether you like it or not. I'm not leaving you here. I don't care who finds me. As long as you're with me—that's all I care about." I slide his sweats up his legs, and once they're on, I move to help him sit up.

The pained look on his face almost causes me to lose it and start sobbing. But if I do that, he'll feel ashamed, and he shouldn't be. His father should be.

I have to stay strong. For Roman.

My hands shake as I gently tug the t-shirt over his head. I take one arm and help it through the armhole. He lets out a pained groan as I take the other. I'm worried he's broken something, but I don't know what. He spins himself and places his feet on the floor.

Roman looks up at me through the curtain of his hair, his big, sad blue eyes cutting me straight to the core. A tear rolls free as I give him a small smile. I push his hair behind his ears and watch as his body shakes with emotion. I step between his legs and gently rest my hand on his back. He lets out a deep sob as he uses one hand to pull me closer, resting his head on my belly.

I run my fingers through his hair and hum for a few moments so I can compose myself. If I don't, I'm going to start crying and may never stop.

"I've got you. You're mine. I told you I will never give up, will never leave you behind again. I promise you this—you're my forever."

We stay like that for a while, his body shaking from crying and the fever and whatever else he's been holding in for so long. I patiently wait while he lets it all out. Finally, he pulls free from my belly, and I wipe my thumbs under his eyes. They are rimmed with red, and he starts to cry again.

"I love you," I whisper as I squat down in front of

him. I place a small kiss on his salty, wet lips. Drawing away, I rest my forehead against his.

Together, we take a few deep breaths, and he whispers, "I've always loved you, Mila."

I smile. It's a little sad, but in the best way. I wipe away another of his tears. I hear his dad banging around out in the other room, then I flinch when he yells.

"Let's go. Let me take you home." I stand and hold out my hand, palm up.

Roman doesn't hesitate to take it. I help him stand, but as his face contorts in pain and he stumbles a little, I have to wrap my arm around his waist to support his weight.

The yelling in the other room grows louder; it sounds like someone's here.

"Roman. Mila," Hunter yells out.

I release a deep breath in relief. In my worry, I forgot to call Hunter to let him know where I was. The girls must have told him I came here. But he didn't call me...oh, shit. I left my phone in the car.

"Hunter," I scream out.

I need him. Roman needs help getting out to the car, and as much as I want to say I'm strong, I'm already struggling with his weight against mine.

I open the bedroom door to see Hunter pushing past Damon.

"Damon, fuck off. We're taking him this time, and

there's nothing you can do." He shoves Damon, who stumbles back into the kitchen.

Hunter rushes to us and takes Roman's weight. "Hey there, Romeo. I got you."

Roman just grunts at Hunter, and it's obvious Hunter called him that in an attempt to get a rise out of him. Roman used to hate when kids called him that in school when we were younger.

I run back into the room to grab the bag I'd packed for him, scanning the room for his phone and wallet. Once I quickly add them to the backpack, I give the room one last look as I walk out, closing the door behind me.

Roman's father is in his face, yelling about money, and I storm out there and shove him. I think he's just as surprised as I am. Fuck, why did I do that? But I don't let him know I'm scared.

"Fuck off. He owes you nothing," I seethe and turn to Roman, who watches his father with a deadly expression.

"Roman, let's go." Hunter pulls him toward the door, and I start to walk with him when I'm yanked back by my hair and I scream, reaching back to the hand as I feel hairs ripping from my skull.

Suddenly, Roman's there, above me, his hand wrapped around his father's throat. "Let. Her. Go." His voice is raspy and deep. Considering the state I found him in, the strength he displays is shocking.

Hunter helps me up and frees me from Damon's grip.

"Stupid little cunt."

I turn just as Damon backhands me. My head whips to the side, my cheek burning from the force. My hand goes to my cheek as tears roll down.

Roman roars as he shoves Damon back, and he goes flying, crashing into the kitchen cabinet. The door hangs, broken. But he doesn't stay down. Damon gets up and charges at Roman, but Hunter steps in, his fist flying into Damon's gut, who doubles over, groaning.

"Come on, let's go." Hunter grabs my hand and wraps his arm around Roman. But he's not moving; he's watching his father. I look back at Damon, and he's holding a knife now.

"You can't take him from me. You can't take my supply, you greedy whore. It's mine. You can get your kicks somewhere else."

I stand frozen. He just called his son his supply. As in, he only cares about Roman because he has money Damon can steal for his drug addiction.

Damon lunges at me with the knife, and I'm caught off-guard. I scream and throw up my right arm to block the hit. He hits my cast with the knife, and his weight pushes me down. There's a scramble as Hunter and Roman pull Damon from me, trying to get the knife away.

There's a lot of yelling as I attempt to pick myself

up. Damon kicks out at me, and I'm thrown back against the wall, hitting my head on something sharp. I pull away, placing my hand back there, and it comes away warm and sticky with blood. My hands shake as I look up at the scene in front of me. It's like everything's being played in slow motion.

Roman has the knife in his hand, and Hunter holds Damon's throat as he lashes out at him. Damon keeps swinging his arms, trying to connect, but he's looking worn down. And when Hunter shoves him back, he lands on his ass, the dirty dishes in the skink clattering, and he just sits there, staring up at them. Giving up a fight he's never going to win.

Roman stumbles toward me, and I scramble up to hug him. I wrap my arms around him as Hunter picks up the bag, calling out, "Come on."

My ears are ringing from the hit to the head, but I don't let go of Roman. He shakes in my arms. When I see movement from the side, and the glint of silver, I scream.

Damon has another knife and he swings. I shove Roman, the knife slicing down and catching my upper left arm as Damon stumbles past us. I look down in shock. A trail of blood trickles down my arm; it's not deep, but I will need stitches. *Fuck.*

"No," Roman cries out as he pulls me toward him, turning just in time to see Damon lunging again with the knife, but Roman hits him in the stomach.

Damon's eyes widen as he looks down to

where Roman's hand sits against his belly. Roman slowly peels his fingers away from the black handle of the knife he'd been holding. I stumble back a little with Roman as I watch Damon drop his knife and grab the one buried deep inside him.

I stand in shock as Hunter rushes back inside after putting the bag in his car and sees the scene for the first time.

"Fuck. *Fuck.*" Hunter looks at me, then Roman.

The cut on my arm throbs as blood trickles down my arm. I look to my hand and see drops of blood on the dirty carpet.

I close my eyes. What do we do? We need to call the cops, and we need help getting Damon to a hospital. The knife's still in; he can survive this. This was self-defense. After all those crime shows I watched, I know they will let Roman off. He was protecting me. I open my eyes and see Damon sputtering blood. *Fuck.*

"Close the door," I say to Hunter. My voice is calm now as I try to remove myself from the situation. If I give in to the fear and anger, I might lose it, and I can't. I need to be strong. We all do.

Hunter doesn't question me—he closes it.

"Fucker, you're going to rot in jail for this," Damon croaks, looking down at the knife.

I watch as he pulls it free, my mouth dropping open as he starts to bleed all over the carpet. The number one rule is to not remove the object. Is he crazy? Does he want to die?

Damon tries to get up and groans. "Call an ambulance."

I hold myself still. I can't move. If I do, I will crumble and I can't do that. I need to be resilient. I need to fix this for Roman.

Roman doesn't say anything; he just wavers beside me. Hunter presses his hand over my arm, and I hiss from the pain. Looking up at him, his big, brown eyes let me know everything will be okay.

But will it?

TWENTY-FIVE

MILA

"**M**ila, we need to go."

Hunter pulls on my arm, but I resist. "We can't. This is a crime scene, and if we leave, Roman is the first person they'll look for."

Roman shakes his head and lets out a strangled cry. I reach for him. "I'm sorry. I'm so sorry."

He just killed his father, and although he'd been defending me, I know that's something he will carry with him for the rest of his life. Even though his father was an asshole, Roman never should have been forced to harm, much less kill, his own flesh and blood.

"I have a record, fighting…they won't believe me." Roman runs his hands down his face, leaving a smear of blood. I think it's mine, but I don't tell him.

"It was self-defense. We were both here. They will

know it was," Hunter reassures him as he pulls out his phone.

Roman grabs it before Hunter can dial any numbers. "No, no. I have to run. I have to leave. They'll lock me up. Everything bad always happens to me." Roman stumbles. His fever has kicked in, and the adrenaline has run out, and he's collapsing in front of me.

My heart breaks.

Everything bad always happens to me.

I look to Damon, who has stopped breathing. It's strange, this out-of-body feeling I get when I see him lying motionless.

"Don't run. Go to Hunter's house. I'll stay here and call the cops. I'll say I stabbed him, that it was self-defense." I point to my arm, then I touch the back of my head where I hit it, and my cheek. I hiss at the pain. It hurts to touch.

"I can't leave you here alone, Mila," Hunter protests. "You can't take the fall; you didn't do this. It was self-defense. I'll say I did it."

"No, Roman's right. Everything bad always happens to him. But starting today, no more. I will say I stabbed Damon. We just need a plan."

I glance around the room—it's a mess. Then I look Hunter over; he's not bleeding. Roman, I do a more thorough inspection of. His hands...does he have any knife wounds? Is he bleeding?

No, thankfully. I shake my head, and the pain hits

me. "Fuck," I grip my head, and Hunter moves to hold me, but I push him away.

"No, don't touch me. Just in case. I need you to take Roman to your house. You need to shower and burn the clothes. Or at least bury them until we can burn them. Where the treehouse was meant to be— take them there. The cops will come question you. So, be the best actors you have ever been."

I look around again, and Hunter nods as he helps Roman up.

"You have to stick to your story. The closest to the truth is always best. I came here because Roman called me. You came because…" I wait for Hunter to answer me.

"Sadie and Cadence told me you got a call from Roman and came here. I tried to call you, but you didn't pick up, so I grew worried."

I nod. "That's what happened. But…my phone was on silent. I didn't hear it ring in my bag when I got here. You came and took Roman in your car. I was leaving just after you and said I would meet you after I went home and changed out of my dress."

"And then what happened? How do you explain why Damon's dead?" Hunter asks, confused.

"You don't know. Why would you? You're taking Roman home to help him. His dad beat him, and he's sick. You're taking care of him at your house."

I watch as he nods slowly, then he looks me in the eye. It clicks. He gets what I'm saying. Hunter doesn't need to know more. If he says anything more, things he shouldn't know, then we will get caught. The rest is up to me.

I count in my head to a hundred and then search the floor where I'd dropped my keys. My head feels like a million bees are buzzing in there and stinging me. I find them and scramble up, not looking over at the body and the pool of blood under it.

I open the trailer door, trying to make sure nothing I do will come back to bite me in the ass if there's an investigation. As I open my car door, I look around, but I don't spot anyone. If someone heard what happened, they didn't even bother to find out what was going on. I reach into the car and grab my bag before closing and locking it.

Each step I take toward the trailer door, I shake a little more. I don't want to go back in there with him. I don't want to be in there with his body. But I also don't want to be out here with whatever lurks in the dark. I close the trailer door behind me and sag against it.

I count slowly to a hundred again and pull my phone out of my bag. There are a ton of missed calls from Hunter, one from Cadence, and two from Sadie.

I ignore them as I dial 9-1-1. My thumb hovers over the call button as I panic again.

Have I done everything right? My phone would be tracked here too. Same as Hunter's. That's why he had to go with Roman. I was here longer.

I look over at the knife covered in blood.

"Fingerprints," I whisper out loud.

The knife doesn't have my fingerprints. It has Roman's and Damon's. *Fuck.* I'm going to have to touch the knife. I'm going to need to cut myself with the knife. So many criminals got caught because they cut their hand when they stabbed someone. Roman didn't, luckily. That's why I checked. But I need this to be believable.

I crawl over to where it lays, my hand shaking as I pick it up with two fingers. I can't wipe off Damon's fingerprints. Mine can't land on top of his either, or they will know I'm lying.

Fuck, fuck. I can't do this. My hands shake so much, I can barely hold the knife as I move it to where I would hold it. I bite the inside of my cheek as I slice my finger. I drop the knife and hold my hand to my chest while I scan the room one last time. The adrenaline has run out as I reach for my phone.

I unlock it, the numbers still glowing up at me, and I press the green call button.

"Nine-one-one, what's your emergency?"

TWENTY-SIX

JACE

ow can he stand to look at her?

Mila Hart killed his dad, and he's holding her hand at his funeral.

His father's fucking funeral. With the girl who killed him!

The turnout is very small, and there is nothing but dry eyes. Damon Valentine wasn't a good man. But the killer...at his funeral. If that isn't a stab in the back—pun intended.

She stabbed him in the back. That's what everyone is saying. I tried to ask Roman and he refused to talk to me. Last week, I thought we were getting better. Closer. But now I see that all it takes to be his friend is to kill his father.

Though the guy was a grade-A asshole, he was Roman's only living relative. That's it. Roman lost everything because she, what? Forgot her phone.

Everything we'd built in the past four years has crumbled in weeks. This was our year for football and girls. Having fun and partying all year. Now, it has all been destroyed by a petite blonde with a wicked tongue.

She uses that tongue to wreck her enemies and lure in her lovers.

Watching the three of them at school has been damn confusing. She kisses Hunter in the hallways; she sits with him at lunch and they're a couple. But she holds Roman's hand in the halls, even when she's kissing Hunter.

Everyone has been talking about it. I knew she said she wouldn't choose between us. But this…it's not what I had in mind.

Everyone starts to leave and Mom pats my shoulder. She came for Roman. She said funerals are not always about the dead, but the living and showing you care for them. Mom has always cared for Roman.

I stand where I am, watching as Mom gives Roman a hug. He accepts it and nods at whatever she's saying to him. Probably telling him to come over for dinner, that she hasn't seen him in a while.

We have a game tonight, and I can't lose. This season has gone from decent to shit. The scouts aren't gonna come to my games. And Grady…there have been rumors about the scholarships he's been offered possibly being taken away. That's total bullshit. But

Mom and Dad have been talking about it when they thought I couldn't hear.

I need the scholarship. I need to get out of this town and make something of myself. Going to the local college here isn't an option. I want to leave the state. Start fresh. I want to go all the way. I want to be drafted into the NFL. I want it all. But I can't have that here.

And without my friends…the ones who supported me through all these years? I can't do it. Hunter, Roman, and I are a team. We work together, unlike other players on our team. Emerson tries, but it's not his end goal to leave here playing football. He gives one hundred percent, but I need more. Hunter and Roman gave everything; they knew, together, we could secure the dream for me, the college for Hunter, and we would have taken Roman with us. I wouldn't have left him behind, even though he doesn't want to go to college.

All three of us against the world.

Now, it's all three of them against the world, and I'm left here drowning without even a life jacket.

I don't confront Roman like I want to. I nod at him and he nods back at me before I turn and leave to get ready for tonight's game.

Alone.

***

The game was a total disaster. Grady, the one guy

everyone can depend on, our captain, lost it, and Coach took him out. After that, the rest of the team shattered, and the game turned into one big clusterfuck.

Seeing that Mila is still up, I knock on her door. Only her car is in the driveway, which surprises me. Where's her dad? More importantly, where are Hunter and Roman?

It's time to fix this shit between us all. I need the guys, but not for the team—fuck football. I need my friends back. I have nothing without them. My whole life, I've had amazing friends, and I didn't realize how lucky I was until I lost it all.

When Mila answers the door, she's wearing that little silk sleep set. The one she wore when she told us all we give her butterflies. I doubt I give her butterflies anymore.

Her eyes are rimmed with red. She's been crying. It gets my back up—why is she crying? She didn't lose her father. She took that life.

And I lose it. "Why did you kill him? He was all Roman had; you knew that. Even if he was a fucking asshole."

She looks at me, the tears now rolling down her face, and I can't stop myself.

"What do you have to say for yourself? I didn't think you had it in you to stab someone in the back. But then, I guess, you're more like your mother than I thought."

She scoffs then shakes her head. So much for the sassy girl I once knew. Can't even talk to me.

"Well?" I prompt, yet again.

She crosses her arms over her chest. "I have nothing to say to you."

Nothing? How can she have nothing to say to me? *Fuck's sake.*

I wanted to get Mila alone to ask her what really happened. Why she would do that. But as soon as I saw her, I unleashed all the anger I had—about the game, about us, about everything—onto her, and I can't stop. It's like the dam has broken and everything is being released. I can't stop it; the water is flowing too fast, and my mind screams with pain.

"Tell me," I yell at her.

I thought things were broken before, but at least they were fixable. If I'm left on the outside, looking in, how can I fix anything? Especially when I don't know what I need to fix. I'm sick of it.

"Fuck off, Jace. If you think you can walk over here and yell at me, like you know everything..." she screams. "You don't know shit. You haven't spoken to Roman or Hunter. So, why would I talk to you?"

"Roman won't talk to me, but I deserve to know," I scream back, unsure of what I wanted to know. This isn't what I had planned.

"Why do you *deserve* to know anything? You spout the same shit everyone else is at school. Isn't that enough for you? Don't you love gossip? Are you calling me a murderer behind my back as I pass you in the halls like so many others? You seem to know everything, so what are you asking me?"

Fuck. I spin on the spot and slam my fist into the wall. *Fuck*. What the hell really happened?

She stands there and glares at me. The Mila I used to know isn't there anymore; she's changed.

Everything.

"You ruined everything when you came back," I yell. The words echo in my head.

"I'm sorry I kissed your brother, Jace. You were with Britney. We weren't a couple; we were barely friends. You made that clear when you had her suck your dick for me to see. I understood loud and clear that you were angry. Everything else...it happened because of your actions. I didn't ruin anything."

Her voice breaks, and I want her to look at me. How can she say that it was all me? It started the day she came back.

Hunter wanted her and now they're this happy couple. Roman...I don't even know where he fits in with them. But he's touching her. He lets her touch him, and I have no idea how she even got him to do that.

I knew she would choose Hunter and Roman over me. Hell, if my brother wasn't gay, she would have chosen him over me too. That's why I invited Britney over and showed Mila I didn't need her. I make my own choices.

I wasn't going to be second best to my brother... again. I'm always one step behind. Grady 2.0, but the original is always better. Fuck, I bet she knew he was gay before me too.

Me and the boys had everything under control. We played amazing football. We hung out all the time. We went to parties. Played dumb drinking games and Xbox until we passed out. Life was perfect...before she came back.

"What do you want from me, Jace?" Her voice was a broken whisper and it has me stepping back.

I peer at my throbbing fist. This isn't why I came here. Why do I get so angry?

"I want everything back to the way it was."

She waits for a moment and looks at me before she answers. "Did you ever apologize to Grady?"

The fuck?

This isn't just about Grady; it's about Hunter and Roman. I don't know how to stop whatever's happening. I can't get Hunter to talk to me unless it's on the field. He refuses to look at me when we pass in the halls. Roman doesn't even grunt at me anymore.

"Did you?"

What? Grady...what has this—Fuck it.

"I said I was sorry, and he just keeps ignoring me." Like everyone in my life does. Even my own parents aren't speaking to me more than they need to. They're angry at me for what went down, but I didn't do anything wrong.

"You said you're sorry and think that fixes everything?" She shakes her head at me like I'm the bad guy.

I know I'm not the bad guy. I didn't out Grady to everyone; that was Britney. I didn't kill someone; that was Mila.

"Britney took something very important from him —his identity. She had no right to do that, and you just let it happen. In front of everyone. Did you ever think to ask him why he didn't tell you? Why his own brother found out the same way everyone else did?"

I don't answer her. I didn't let it happen—it happened all on its own. What was I supposed to do? If I'd known, then at least there was a chance I could have stopped her. I guess I was surprised and didn't know what to say.

"Because he wasn't ready." She throws her hands up. "It was his choice. If he wanted to tell you. Or everyone. Or no one at all. That's his choice. He makes it and only him."

"I don't know what to do," I say, defeated. I came over here for answers.

Why did she kill Roman's dad?

Why is Hunter kissing her against her locker, and why is Roman holding her hand like he can't *not* be touching her?

Yet, all she wants to talk about is my brother.

Fuck that. I want to know what really happened.

"You need to fix what's broken between you and your brother. Go to Grady and just listen to him. Even if he's not ready to talk, sit beside him and show him you care. I know he's hurting. He hates that there's a rift between you, and I hate that for you too."

Did she tell him that? Why does he talk to her and not me? I apologized, and I meant it. I'm sorry that it happened.

"If I do that, will you tell me why you killed Roman's dad?"

Mila shakes her head at me and steps back into her house. "Talking and listening to your brother needs no reward, other than the reward of understanding and accepting him."

"Fuck this." I turn to leave. This didn't help at all.

If anything, I'm more confused.

TWENTY-SEVEN
MILA

t's been three weeks since that night in the trailer. It's been hard. Turns out, people treat you differently when you've taken a person's life, even in self-defense. I'm just glad Roman doesn't have to go through this. I don't think he would have survived it.

Thankfully, the investigation didn't last long. The police believed my story. Hell, given the state Roman was in when they went to question him, they didn't question him long over what had gone down. They believed that I forgot my phone and went back for it. Damon attacked me with the knife, and I grabbed it in self-defense, accidentally killing him.

But it sits there between us and the world.

The lie.

It makes us stronger, but if it was to get out, it would destroy us.

I'm being called a murderer in the halls. Roman hates it; he wants to hurt every person who gossips about me. The only thing keeping him from doing that is my touch. If I'm touching him, he knows I'm safe and with him.

That's how the rumors started. Ones I knew would surface if Roman became my boyfriend. He's not; he hasn't wanted to talk about us, and I won't push him. After what just happened, we can wait as long as we all need before we put a label on anything.

He's happy with us all being together as friends right now. I will take Roman any way I can, and if I get to hold his hand all day and keep him safe, I'm more than happy for the status quo.

Roman is still worried. He's scared we will be caught and all go to jail. I think it will take time until everything's behind us. The school counselor set up Roman and I with therapists to talk to, but it isn't really helping.

Having to keep the lie is exhausting. Having to lie to my dad has been the hardest thing I've ever done. But I can't tell him the truth. If anyone knows what really happened, it could get out and cause even more problems for Roman, Hunter, and me.

As I reach my front door, there are red roses on the porch.

Every Saturday, without fail, I get red roses...one more each week. Today, there are five waiting for me, and I look over to Jace's house. Why would he bother with roses when the last time he spoke to me he just yelled and asked me why I killed Roman's father?

The Rebels won last night's game against the Knights. Roman and Hunter played like I'd never seen before. They were unstoppable. Jace played a good game too, and Grady seemed happier. He'd sent me a text last night saying, "Thank you." I wasn't sure what it was for, but I'm just relieved to see him more himself.

I hold the roses to my chest as I unlock the door, feeling uneasy. Dad made me promise I would always have someone with me, and I told him Hunter would be with me, but his dad came home to talk about Roman living there full time.

Roman's been living there since it all happened. Hunter's mom said he can stay, but I think for Roman to stay they needed to go through Child Protective Services, and Hunter said his dad had to come back for that. It happened today, so I've been at Sadie's house.

I needed a distraction and having her tell me the story of the night of the homecoming dance again is the best medicine. Not only did she get her dance with Tyler, she's been on a few dates with him, and they kissed last night at the game.

At least she doesn't treat me differently. She hasn't asked me about what happened, but she told me she doesn't believe the school gossip.

Why would I stab someone in the back? I bet Britney started that. That's her favorite move.

"Hey, Mila."

I look up and see Makai waving over at me. I wave back with a smile. "How are you?" I ask. No one has figured out that he's the guy Britney caught kissing Grady. I've seen him over visiting Grady more this week. More study sessions, I guess? So cute.

"I'm good. Do you have a secret admirer?" He looks at the roses, and I smile.

"I guess so. It's not Hunter or Roman." I don't add that they both think it's Jace. I don't want Jace to know that we've caught on. Not yet at least. Things with him have been less...tense.

Hunter said that he'd spoken to Jace. That he'd mended some of the hurt between them. Roman didn't tell me much, but after last night's game, I was glad to see the smiles on their faces. Even Jace's.

"Did you want to come hang?" Makai offers, and I shake my head and smile.

"No, I'm actually just going to grab some stuff and go over to my dad's girlfriend's place. They have a hot tub, and it's calling my name."

Since I got my cast off two weeks ago, that's all I want to do. I just haven't had the time to do it this week. Until now.

"Okay, see you tomorrow," he says as he gives me a shy smile. He's so cute. Go Grady.

I get inside my house, put the roses in some water, grab what I need for tonight, and jump back in my car.

***

"Hey, good looking. You want anything?" Walker calls from the kitchen as I pass on my way to the hot tub.

I pause in the doorway and see he's dripping water from his board shorts onto the tiles. "Kate's gonna yell at you." I point at the puddle he's made while standing at the refrigerator.

He gives me his cocky grin and winks. "She will be dazzled by my smile and forget all about it."

I laugh and shake my head. He's so full of himself, and he knows it. "You wanna bet on that? Should I call her in here now and see which one of us wins?"

As I pretend to go get Kate, his warm arms wrap around my bare waist and he lifts me up, spinning me around before planting my ass on the kitchen counter. He takes a step back and looks over my body. I smack him on the chest, and he chuckles.

"Hot stuff, if you're gonna be wearing that tiny red bikini, I need to check you out." He lets out a whistle. "You sure your heart's set on Hunter?"

With a laugh, I shove him again as he starts to show off his biceps, like that will change my mind.

"I'm very sure it's not wanting you and your big ego."

"One night with me, Mila." His wily grin has me rolling my eyes. "And you will change your mind about my big *ego*."

He grabs a towel and mops up the water from the floor as I hop down, fixing my bikini before making my way outside. I don't want to be in the same room as Walker's big...anything.

Madison's out here with her friend Bella. They made up with each other, and I've met her a few times this week. I guess her spending more time here means I will see more of her. They're sitting on some deck chairs as I wave over at them.

Madison jumps up and runs over, hugging me. "So glad you're here. It's weird with Walker always here."

I hug her back. "Just ignore him. He loves it," I tell her, and she giggles. "I promise."

I hear water splashing from the hot tub and look over to see Asher watching me. *Fuck.* He's reclined back, a soda can in his hand, and he gives me a small smile and nod hello. I do the same in return. That's been pretty much the only thing we've said to each other in weeks.

"Want to come in the hot tub with me?" I practically beg Madison. She shakes her head and shrinks down a little as Walker comes strolling out, food and drinks in his arms.

"He doesn't bite," I reassure her, but Walker must hear me.

"Only in the best ways, I promise."

My mouth drops open. He didn't just say that to Madison.

Asher catches it, and I hear him yelling, "That's my sister, dick." Walker says he's joking. He better be, or I will go over there right now and junk-punch him.

I haven't been around Asher like this since he admitted he wants to be more than my *friend*. Not to mention the butterflies thing I get around him.

Which is only worse now that he hasn't exactly spoken to me. I don't know how to fix this. Are the butterflies just because I'm anxious around him now? Or is it because something is still there and I don't know how to process it? I don't know if he's giving me space because of what he said, or if he's worried about what I will say. I just need a night off from everything and to have a little fun.

Hunter and Roman are meeting me here, but I don't know how long it will take them to show up. Fuck.

"Come on, Mila, or I will bite your ass," Walker calls from the hot tub, and I roll my eyes at Madison. Her cheeks are pink, and I nod for her to go back to Bella.

"If you bite my ass, I will punch you right in your ego," I reply before I turn around.

Asher has Walker in a headlock. They're splashing around a bit, and it's the perfect distraction for me to get in and not have them watch me.

I dip my toes in the hot water and moan at the warmth. It's so good, I want to live in here. I submerge my whole body, my head just above the water, close my eyes, and sigh as I tilt my head back.

It's grown quiet suddenly, so I open my eyes and bring my head up to find Asher and Walker staring at me. They're not even moving; it's like they're just stuck.

I frown. "Hey." I splash a little bit of water at them.

Walker blinks. Asher shifts and looks away. And it makes the butterflies rise up. No, not tonight. Shut that shit down, stupid body. Walker sees the change in Asher and gives me that cocky grin. "Fucker," I mutter under my breath, and his eyes light up.

"Just one night, Mila. You, me...my *ego*. We'll rock your world." Walker licks his lips and winks.

Asher's watching him like he can't believe Walker's propositioning me in the hot tub with him right there.

Feeling light and free, I laugh. I know Walker's messing with me...well, partly. I'm sure if I said yes, he would throw me over his shoulder like a caveman and run off with me to show me the big "ego" he claims to possess. But he does it to fuck with me. And I love how our friendship is so easy. Carefree.

I haven't felt like this in weeks; everyone tiptoes around me like I'm this crazy killer girl or I'm some fragile flower. Walker acts like everything is the same, like nothing's changed. It makes me happy.

Standing up in the water, I twirl, letting him see me again before bending down close to him. His eyes widen, and I can see the shock in them, like maybe this one time I will take him up on his offer.

I smirk and bop his nose with my finger. "In your dreams, quarterback." I poke my tongue out at him and return to where I'd been sitting.

He groans, and I watch his hand tug on his board shorts under the water. It makes me smile. Yep, this is normal. This is what teenagers do. Not sit around and dwell on things they can't change. They wait for their boys to come and have fun teasing the quarterback for the rival team.

"You're a flirt, Mila." He pouts at me.

I chuckle. "You love it."

And he nods and points at me.

This is our usual game, and I'm just happy that he still wants to play it with me. Asher doesn't say anything; he just watches the exchange between us. I finally relax when they start talking about last night's game and I can just chill out here while I wait.

"Hey, babe."

I open my eyes and Hunter's there, stripping down to get in. Roman's eyes are on Asher. He doesn't seem to like him; neither does Hunter. But the whole time I've been in here, Asher hasn't spoken to me, so they have nothing to worry about.

"How'd it go?"

I've been a little worried about Hunter's dad possibly saying no to Roman living there and all the paperwork and stuff involved. It would be easier for him to let Roman go to a group home. And I know Hunter's dad isn't a family man.

"Roman gets to stay." Hunter smiles. It doesn't reach his eyes, but when he sees me staring he grins, just as he jumps into the hot tub with his boxers on.

I laugh as he kisses me then looks behind him to Walker, wiggling his ass at him. Walker smacks it, and they laugh. At least they're still on good terms.

Roman hesitates outside the hot tub. I reach out and hold his hand. He gives me a small smile.

"Did you want to come in? Or I can get out and we can go watch a movie?"

Preferably at my house.

With the three of us.

Alone.

TWENTY-EIGHT
MILA

Nothing says late-night snack like when you're the snack.

We left Kate's house and made our way back to mine. Hunter put on a movie and Roman lingered beside me, everywhere I went. Like he's worried if he can't see me, something will happen.

Considering how often he does that, I'm starting to take it seriously. Those guys who beat him up and hit me with their car...I think that's who he's referring to when he says he can't be with me. To keep me safe. But when he's with me, he watches me like a hawk, and that's not healthy either.

I met some of the Sons of Death MC at Damon's funeral, and I have to say, they're really good guys. Pinkie is a crack up. I know they have Roman's best interests at heart, and they only want the best for him.

They're a little intimidating and scary...but in a hot, bad boy way. I can see the appeal to join and for the ladies who chase them.

But I don't need one. I have my own bad boy. He just needs time before I can officially call him mine.

I'm making popcorn and grab the bowl out the cabinet. I feel Hunter press up behind me, his hand wrapping around my belly, and his fingers dancing under my tee on my bare skin. I press back into him and look up. He grins before spinning me and walking me backward until my ass hits the counter.

"You're happy tonight," he says, and I smile.

I am happy. He winks as he grips under my ass and lifts me onto the counter, pushing my legs apart and standing between them.

Hunter reaches up to my hair tie—my hair is in a messy bun—and pulls it free. I shake it out so that it flutters around my cheeks.

"I love your hair down."

I raise a brow. As though I didn't already know that. He's forever touching my hair.

He grabs my chin and captures my mouth with his. My back arches into him. I want to feel him against me. We haven't done more than kiss in weeks; it's all been too much to think about more. But I want my life back. I want us all to start again. I need him, and I want Roman.

Tonight, I want it all.

He breaks the kiss and looks over to Roman, who's now left the couch and is watching us. I don't know how he'll react to this. He's watched me and Hunter kiss. But this—what I'm planning on doing—is a lot more than kissing Hunter.

I reach out to Roman, and Hunter steps away from me, giving Roman room if he wants to come and kiss me. But also giving him the option to walk away. I would never push him to do something he doesn't want to.

He takes a step forward, and I can't stop the smile crossing my face. Stopping, he looks to Hunter then me.

"You don't have to do anything you don't want," I tell him. "You can watch us, or we can leave the room. You're in control here, Roman. This is new to all of us, but it's up to you how far you want to take it. I'll always be here for you, no matter what."

I want him to know that. No matter what he chooses, I'm still here.

He nods, and Hunter pulls me from the counter and spins me so he's at my back and Roman is facing me.

Roman pushes his hair back, watching as Hunter lifts the hem of my sleep tee. It's loose and baggy, and I'm not wearing anything else under there.

"Isn't she beautiful, Roman?" Hunter's voice is

deep as he lifts the tee over my head, and I'm standing there, topless, as he cups one of my breasts.

I push my ass into Hunter. I'm needy and want to be touched. I can feel his cock, hard against my ass, and I rub against it. He moans in my ear and plucks at my nipple.

"You want to play with her nipples?" he whispers across the room to Roman.

There's a flash of heat in his eyes as he covers the distance between us in less than a second. I'm taken by surprise. I think Hunter is too since he stills behind me.

Roman's hand wraps around my throat and he tilts my head back. My eyes meet his, and he watches me as he runs his thumb over my bottom lip, and I lick the pad of his thumb. He presses on my lower lip, and I gasp, opening my mouth to him.

My heart beats loudly in my ears. Roman's eyes burn into mine as I reach up and hold his wrist. He flinches a little at my touch but allows me to hold it.

I pull it forward and suck his thumb into my mouth; my tongue swirls around it, and he lets out a deep groan. I try not to smile, but it's almost impossible as he presses his hard body against mine and grinds himself against my belly. He's hard and hot. My heart is racing as my breathing picks up.

When I came home with them both tonight, the last place I expected to be was sandwiched between them. And I'm not disappointed at all. From behind me, Hunter grabs my hips and grinds his arousal into my ass. I tilt my head back and to the side as his lips graze over my neck. I shudder in response to his touch.

"I'm gonna taste you," Hunter whispers into my ear. When he bites my lobe, pleasure tingles down between my thighs.

"Do you want to taste Roman?" he purrs into my hair.

My eyes meet Roman's again, and he pulls his thumb free and wipes my lips with it.

"I want to taste him," I reply on a moan.

Roman watches me, his breath hitching as I use my fingertips to gently touch his chest. He's wearing a tee, so I'm not touching his skin directly, and if that makes him more comfortable, then it works for me.

"Do you want that, Roman? You want Mila's lips wrapped around your hard cock while I eat her pussy?"

I like how Hunter's taken control here. It's easier for me to concentrate on Roman's needs—where I can touch him, cues to see what's too much—if I don't have to think about everything else. I don't know how he did stuff with other girls before me, but we will learn this together.

Roman doesn't answer Hunter. Instead, he kisses me. His lips are warm and soft as he wraps his hand around my hair and pulls me to his mouth. Hunter doesn't move away, but he loosens his grip on me and lets Roman have this kiss.

I reach up and very softly place my hand on his cheek and he presses into it. Smiling, I pull him to me, our tongues dancing as I try to find some friction for the need pulsing between my thighs.

With Hunter whispering words of encouragement to us both, I press my chest into Roman, and he doesn't back away.

We pull apart, and the kiss has left me dizzy in the best way as I blink and look into Roman's eyes. He smiles, and my heart melts right there.

"I love you," I tell him, wanting him to know how much I love him.

His eyes glisten at my words. "I love you too," he murmurs softly.

I place my hand back on his chest, my palm over his heart. This time, the reaction is different. He smiles and places his hand there too. Releasing a deep breath, he closes his eyes.

When he opens them, he nods at Hunter. What does that mean? I don't get a chance to ask since Hunter flips me around and over his shoulder, slapping me on the ass. I squeal at the sudden movement, but it doesn't take long before I'm dropped onto the sofa bed, and Hunter's looking down at me with that predatory glare of his.

Roman comes over and lies down beside me. I reach over and take his hand and he smiles.

"Roman?" Hunter asks. At first, I think he's going to say more but realize he's just prompting Roman to speak up.

"I want you to touch me, Mila," Roman whispers. His eyes drop to my chest then back into my eyes.

He's giving me permission to touch him, and I nod, trying not to scare him away with my excitement. "If it's too much, just say so. Okay? No judgment; just say stop, and I will. You can even guide my hands to where you're okay with my touch."

He grunts and I giggle. That's my Roman.

I move to the hem of his tee and tug it up. He lets me and then removes it himself, looking back over at me. His chest is so sexy, and I know it's a massive no-go zone normally, so I'm going to take my time and ease him into it all.

Getting up on my hands and knees, I crawl over to him. He lies flat against the mattress, and I watch his jaw tick. I don't like that. He should be turned on and excited, not stressed.

"Roman," I whisper. "Would it be easier if I told you what I'm about to do? That way you can choose to stop it before it happens?" I watch as he lets out a deep breath and nods. He's still a little tense, but baby steps.

Tonight is his first lesson that touch can be more than pain. It can be pleasure too.

"I'm going to kiss you. Then kiss your chest, right here." I point between his pecs. "Then slowly kiss my way down to here." I point at the edge of his shorts. I can see the bulge in there—he wants this, that much is clear. Just, getting there is slightly different than how I would with Hunter.

I turn to see Hunter walking up the stairs. He pauses for a moment and smiles, nodding at me before blowing me a kiss.

He's giving us this time alone. I wonder if this is something they talked about in advance. I like that Hunter's giving us this special moment together.

I wait for Roman to say stop, but he hasn't. He looks at me expectantly.

I kiss his mouth, then tenderly kiss his chest. I watch his eyes; they're on mine as my hands stay on the mattress, not touching him with anything but my lips. I work my way down, and he moans as I get to the edge of his shorts.

Deciding to take a chance, I show him my hand moving to the bulge in his shorts. I wait for him to say something, and his eyes only grow more heated as I press my palm against him.

Roman's moan fills the room and it has me moaning with him as it goes right to my core. I feel hot all over as I lick my lips.

"I'm going to pull your shorts—" Before I can even finish, Roman scrambles and takes everything off, and I try not to laugh at how enthusiastic he is. I didn't expect that to happen.

I sit back and look him over. Fuck, he's absolutely

perfect in every way. I forget to ask him and palm his heavy cock. He jerks under my hand but doesn't tell me to stop as I wrap my fingers around it and leisurely stroke it a couple of times, enjoying the reaction on his face. He always holds himself so stiff and expressionless. But with his cock in my hand, he can't give me the poker face.

"I'm going to lick and taste you." My voice is deep and husky.

His breathing speeds up, but he doesn't immediately respond, so I wait. I have to be sure he's ready.

"I want your mouth on my cock," he finally says, and I need that just as much as he does.

I lean forward, wishing I had my hair tie, but I hold my hair back as best I can as I lick the tip of his cock, swirling my tongue around as I look up to him. He watches me as his hands grip the sheets. I love his reaction; I could do this all day just to watch him so worked up.

I stroke my hand up his length and suck the tip of his cock.

"Fuck, oh shit," he mutters, and I smile around his cock as I decide to take his length deeper.

He pulls my hair away from my face, and I look up at him, his cock in my mouth, and he moans my name. The look he gives me has me squeezing my thighs together.

His cock I can touch without any issues.

Maybe I can touch him while he's feeling this

pleasure. I caress his hip gently, and he doesn't move. I hold it slightly tighter, and his body stills under mine. I let go, swirling my tongue around his cock, and he mutters a string of curse words before he groans, his hips flexing up to meet my strokes.

I use my other hand to play with his balls, and I feel them tighten as his body bows towards me.

"Mila, fuck," is the only warning I get before his hot cum shoots into my mouth, and I swallow his cock, chasing the taste of him and loving that he let me do this.

Breaking free, I look over at him. He breathes deeply, and the grin he gives me has me rubbing my thighs together, wanting friction.

He opens his mouth, then closes it, like he has no words.

"Speechless? Glad I could blow your mind." I'm not sure how he would feel if I kissed him. Some guys find tasting themselves a turn-off.

He shakes his head and lets out a deep chuckle. "That was amazing, Mila. I had no idea...no idea that's how it felt."

I'm just about to tell him that's because it's me sucking his cock when I see it written on his face. Something I'd never considered, only making sense to me now.

The no touching, watching him at that first party I crashed, everyone all over each other and Roman avoiding the only other girl in the room.

Hunter left us and gave us privacy.

Is Roman a virgin? No. There's no way.

"Was that your first time?" I ask hesitantly, not wanting to ruin this moment by asking him.

He nods, and I watch his Adam's apple bob as he sits up a little. He reaches for me. I move up and kiss him. He reaches for my head and pulls me in closer.

"I saved all my firsts for you, Mila."

I'm stunned. Holy shit.

He moves around so he hovers over me and he gives me a wicked grin. I have a feeling where this is going and it's gonna be good.

He traces a path of kisses down my breasts and chest, and the butterflies fly wild in my belly, before he stops at the waistband of my shorts. He looks up at me and I smile. He doesn't need permission. I'm about soaked through, I want what he can give me, and when the corner of his lip quirks, I know I'm in for a good time.

Without warning, my shorts and panties are gone and Roman's face is between my thighs. His warm tongue laps out at my clit and I moan. I grab his hair carefully, but fuck…I need to hold on for this ride.

I open my thighs and he licks me before his fingers start to explore. If this is a first time, he is doing amazing. He slips two fingers inside of me and I can feel him trying to find my g-spot.

His mouth sucks on my clit and I don't get a chance to show him where my g-spot is before I'm bucking off the bed and calling out his name. The pressure never lets up and I ride out my orgasm on his mouth.

I tap him. "I need a break." My body is so sensitive, I shake from the aftershocks of that and the pleasure's only amplified knowing that was the first time he's ever done that and I got to be another of his firsts.

We snuggle up together. I don't touch his chest but it's perfect.

TWENTY-NINE
MILA

I wake up between Hunter and Roman, still unable to believe what Roman told me last night.

Everything was perfect. I got my happy ending— I got a much better one when Roman said he saved all his firsts for me. We lay together, snuggling, and Hunter must have made his way down to sleep behind me at some point.

There's a knock at the door, and I groan. Why would I give this up? My little cocoon of happiness. The knocking grows a little louder and Roman bolts upright, and I gasp at the sudden movement. It scared me.

When he looks down, his eyes widen at the sight of me, and he scans the room.

"Fuck, Roman, are you okay?" Hunter asks from

behind me. He gets up and stands beside the bed, looking Roman over.

Roman finally blinks and nods, and I see his shoulders start to relax. I stretch out my hand, palm up, and he looks down at it before taking it.

"Lie down," I tell him. I don't like seeing him like this. Whoever's at the door better have a good reason for waking us up so early on a Sunday morning.

He does, and I snuggle up to him as the knocking starts again.

"I'm coming," Hunter yells and I mutter, "Not yet," as he makes his way over to the door, wearing his black boxers that hug his ass so nice, I want to bite it. I smile to myself at the thought and hold Roman's hand tighter.

The door opens and we hear Jace's voice on the other side. I groan. Fucker, messing up my sleep and scaring Roman like that. Shit, I don't know if that's something Roman will ever grow out of, or if loud sounds like that will always have him on alert.

"Hey, I was wondering if I could talk to you, Roman, and Mila."

I tilt my head to see Jace at the door. His eyes meet mine, and I look away. Roman squeezes my arm and kisses my forehead.

"Mila." Hunter's beside me, holding my sleep tee in his hand. I look down and realize I'm topless still.

"Yeah, okay. Just let me put this on."

Roman helps me, and I smile over at him.

"Thank you." I kiss his lips quickly before sitting up and preparing for this conversation I know has been coming. With the guys being so at ease with Jace this week and the game on Friday, I knew they'd made a step toward being friends again.

Jace comes in and sits on the coffee table while Hunter takes up his position beside me.

He looks at the three of us. "So, you're all together then?" he asks, and it's not what I thought he would lead with, but Jace seems to have a habit of speaking before thinking.

"Yeah, we are. We told you how it was and that you had to accept it before we could accept you back." Hunter shifts beside me, and I reach for his hand. He takes it, and Jace's eyes follow the movement. "You said it was cool."

"I'm cool with it. Just, I guess seeing it like this…I get it."

I wait for him to say more, but he doesn't. So I jump into the conversation. "Since you're here, then that must mean you talked to Grady?"

He dips his head and fiddles with the hem of his shorts before looking back at me. "Yeah, I did. What you said…I didn't want to listen. I was angry—at myself and the world. Not you, Mila. I took everything out on you, and I see how many mistakes I've made because I don't think about my actions.

"I take things out on the people I care about, and I hate that I did that. I'm here to tell you I'm sorry."

When I nod, he lets out a deep breath.

"I'm sorry for lashing out at you over the kiss with Grady. That wasn't fair of me. I shouldn't have been upset. I asked you, you were honest with me, and I wasn't with you. I was hurt. All my life, I've come in second to Grady. No fault of his own, just when you're so close in age, you're always compared to your older brother.

"You were mine, my friend, my first crush, first kiss…When it came to you, I didn't have to share the spotlight with Grady. I was first in your eyes. So, when the two of you kissed, I couldn't see that. I was angry and did the worst thing possible to hurt you."

He did. Anyone but Britney. He used her to get back at me, and he knew she'd been a bitch to me since I returned.

"I don't know if you can ever forgive me for that, but I'm truly sorry."

I shuffle to sit more upright. Crossing my legs, I look over to Jace. His head is tilted to the side, and he looks sincere. He looks beat down and like shit. But he's hit rock bottom, that's how you're supposed to look.

Now it's up to me to forgive him. For us to go back to the way we were…with a few scars left behind to remind us that life isn't perfect. And we all fight.

"I forgive you, Jace."

His eyes widen in shock. He probably wasn't

expecting that. But I need this, for me more than him. I hate that there's been this huge divide between us all, and I seem to be the only one who hasn't forgiven him here.

"You need to work on your anger. Think before you act. Speak up when you're feeling hurt, and we can talk it out."

With a nod, he gives me a beaming smile. He instantly seems lighter at my words, and I smile in return.

"Thank you, Mila. I won't ever abuse your trust again."

It's on the tip of my tongue to tell him not to make promises he can't keep. But I want to give him the benefit of the doubt. He changed so much in the four years I was away. And now we're all changing together. Growing into who we're meant to be.

"Let's go to Annie's Diner for lunch," Hunter suggests.

"Lunch?" I asked, puzzled.

"Yeah, it's noon, babe." He kisses my shoulder and reaches for his shorts.

My stomach rumbles at the thought of food, and I realize I'm hungry. Everyone laughs, and I do too. "Lunch, it is."

***

I laugh at a joke Hunter makes as we walk up the path to my door with food for the night. We spent time down at Annie's Diner with Jace and Roman. It's weird having Jace back. And it's not the Jace I met when I got here. This is more like old Jace. A mix of our childhood but in a grown body.

There, on my doorstep, are six red roses. The hell? I look over to Jace's house and back to the roses.

"He's trying to show me up," Hunter says with a chuckle.

"He needs to stop. I've forgiven him. We're friends now." It might not be what it used to be, but I'm willing to try again. Baby steps. But when did he get the chance to put them there? We left him at the diner. Roman drove himself and left a few minutes behind us.

Hunter wiggles his brows at me, and we make our way inside with all the food and roses.

"I think he wants to be more than friends." He slaps my ass, and I jump.

I chuckle and grab his hoodie, pulling him in for a kiss, squishing the roses between us. He grabs my waist as he plants one right on me.

"Can I eat your pussy for dinner?" Hunter groans into my neck.

"No, you can have it for dessert," I let him know. We don't have time. I want dinner first. Roman wouldn't care if he walked in on us. But I want to see if maybe I can have them both? A Hunter-Roman sandwich.

And speak of the devil.

"Hey, handsome," I call out to Roman as he locks the front door and rushes to the window. We're one step behind him. What's going on? There's a car outside on the street and they're just sitting there with their headlights directed at my house. They slowly peel out and I can see the men from here. My heart sinks as they point at us.

Roman warned me they would find him...find me. I start to shake as Roman grabs the roses from my hand and roars. It's primal and a warning to them.

"Amato family," he spits out.

Roman's phone goes off with a message and we all look down as he opens it.

Amato Assholes: You owe us a fight. Get ready for tonight or your girlfriend gets to fight...for her life.

I have lost feeling in my whole body as it starts to shut down.

They know where I live.

GET THE GAME

Freaking butterflies…

https://books2read.com/thegamebelleharper

BELLE'S BOOKS

REBELS OF RIDGECREST HIGH

Reverse Harem ~ Enemies to Lovers

The Pact

The Lie

The Game

The Win

OMEGAVERSE STANDALONE SERIES

Reverse Harem ~ Standalone

Harley

Storm ~ coming 2024

PARANORMAL REVERSE HAREM

NEW MOON SERIES ~LEXI~

Twice Bitten

Blood Moon

Rising Sun

FULL MOON SERIES ~ADA~

Fallen Wolf

Torn Mate

Shifting Sun

PACK KIBA NOVELS/NOVELLAS

Midnight Prince

Shadow Wolf

CONTEMPORARY STANDALONES

Naughty and Nice ~Christmas Novella

The Christmas Dunk ~ Coming November 2024

ABOUT THE AUTHOR

Belle is an Artist, Author, Wife and Mother.

She has an addiction to reading, notebooks, coloured pens and mint chocolate. She lives in the beautiful Australian bush, surrounded by wildlife and the smell of eucalyptus trees.

She also has a strong love for all 60's music, believes she was born in the wrong era and should have been at Woodstock.

If you would like to find out more about Belle, please come like and follow her:

Click Here to Like Belle's Facebook Page

Join Belle in her Facebook Group

Visit my website HERE

Sign up to my Newsletter to keep up to date with my new Releases, Free Books and Giveaways.

Sign Up HERE